"Caterina—" A~~~~~ the shadows.

"What is it?" Cat asked thinly. "What do you want?"

"To be alone with my wife." A small smile lingered on his incredibly sexy mouth.

Cat drew in a ragged breath. "So you finally remembered my existence. It took you long enough—two months by my reckoning."

"*Cara*—I admit my absence was regrettable, but it really was necessary if—"

"I'm sure it was," she said, cutting him off. "Business, was it?"

He pulled her hard against him and she gasped as she tried to pull in enough air to enable her to tell him to stop this pretense, but all that emerged was a tiny despairing groan.

"Don't be sad, *cara*," he said, obviously mistaking that distressed sound for something else entirely.

And as he murmured soft words of comfort in Italian, he sounded so sincere that she could almost believe he cared.

Diana Hamilton

HIS CONVENIENT WIFE

ITALIAN HUSBANDS

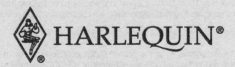

HARLEQUIN®

TORONTO • NEW YORK • LONDON
AMSTERDAM • PARIS • SYDNEY • HAMBURG
STOCKHOLM • ATHENS • TOKYO • MILAN • MADRID
PRAGUE • WARSAW • BUDAPEST • AUCKLAND

ISBN 0-373-12431-7

HIS CONVENIENT WIFE

First North American Publication 2004.

Copyright © 2002 by Diana Hamilton.

This edition published by arrangement with Harlequin Books S.A.

www.eHarlequin.com

Printed in U.S.A.

PROLOGUE

'YOU can't be serious! Are you actually suggesting I marry this Aldo Patrucco character?' Cat's green eyes flashed withering scorn in her grandfather's direction. She pulled herself up to her full five feet nine inches, towering above him, her patrician nostrils pinched with a mix of disbelief and outrage.

Gramps looked oddly shrunken, his clothes suddenly seeming too big for his frail bones as he sat in his favourite armchair. She felt sorry for him, of course she did, very sorry, and she loved him dearly, but no way would she fall in with the insane suggestion he'd just thrown at her.

'Listen to yourself, won't you?' she pushed out through her teeth. 'You're asking me to sell myself—it's positively medieval!'

'And you are overreacting as usual, Caterina,' Domenico Patrucco objected flatly, his black eyes immediately softening in his lined face as he went on to ask gently, 'Why don't you pour the tea and then we can sit and have a civilised discussion? Without shouting.'

Cat let out a long, pent-up breath. It would cost her nothing to humour him, would it? Poor old Gramps had had a tough time recently. He had lost both his

5

sister Silvana and his beloved wife Alice in the space of three months. She and Gramps were still grieving for Alice, so she knew how he felt. She'd never met her Italian great-aunt Silvana, of course, but she knew how much Gramps had looked forward to those long, gossipy letters which had told him of the doings of the Italian side of the family he had split from all those long years ago.

He was all alone now apart from Bonnie, who had been housekeeper here from the year dot. It had been Bonnie who had waddled over to the converted barn in what had once been the stack yard, where Cat had her workshop beneath her living quarters, to announce that her grandfather wished her to join him for afternoon tea.

As she dealt with the tea things Cat wondered if she should offer to move back into the farmhouse to keep the old man company. To stop him brooding and being too lonely. The farmland had been sold off years ago, when he'd retired, and the poor old guy had nothing to do with his time but come up with manic suggestions.

She owed him big time. He and Gran had brought her up since his only child, her mother, had been killed with Cat's father in a road accident when she had been little more than a baby. Their love and care had been unstinting.

Two years ago when she'd left college with a degree in jewellery and silversmithing her grandparents had offered her the use of the barn as a workshop and had reluctantly agreed to her plan to move out of the main house and convert the barn's upper storey into a self-contained flat. She'd been twenty-one and eager to have her own space where she could work or relax, entertain her friends, as the mood took her, be independent.

Keeping him company, keeping an eye on him for a few months, just until he was more himself, wouldn't hurt her. It was, she supposed, the least she could do after all he and Gran had done for her.

The tea poured, she handed him a delicate china cup and saucer and flopped down on the opposite side of the hearth to where he was sitting, her long jeans-clad legs stretched out in front of her, and offered brightly, 'Why don't I move back in here for a month or two? We could spend time together.'

She could sub-let her booth in the craft centre for three months and put her work on hold, she mentally sacrificed, and because that was not the best idea in the world as far as her career was concerned she flashed him a brilliant, Gramps-deluding smile. 'We could take days out together; I'll drive you wherever you want to go—'

'And give me a heart attack!' he interrupted drily. 'The way you drive is as flamboyant and erratic as the way you dress!' And, seeing the way her vivid, animated and lovely features went blank, her wide mouth compressing, he amended gently, 'I thank you for your concern, but I assure you I am not in need of such a sacrifice. What you can do to make me a happy man is give serious consideration to my suggestion.'

So they were back to that, were they? Cat ground her teeth together. Her diversionary tactics hadn't worked, so the only way to handle this was to get it all out in the open, force him to see that his intention to marry her off to his great-nephew was a complete non-starter.

'If your suggestion had been remotely sane I might have done that,' she came back carefully, tenaciously holding on to her patience. 'But I'm willing to listen while you try to say something sensible on the subject; that's all I can promise.'

Leaning back in her chair, she pushed her untameable mane of chestnut hair away from her face. The room was unbearably warm. It was only mid-September but a huge log fire was burning in the hearth. Her grandfather had lived in cool, misty England for many years but his Italian blood still craved warmth.

His heavily hooded eyes held hers but he said nothing for long moments. Trying to find a form of words that would make something crazy sound completely sensible, she guessed. Well, it wouldn't work, however he dressed it up.

'Family,' he said at last. 'It all comes down to family. Forget the shares for the moment; they are important but not as important as closing the circle.'

Cat could have asked him what he meant by that

but didn't bother. And as for the shares she would happily forget them. Forever.

Growing up she'd heard the story so many times it bored her socks off. How her grandfather had been incensed, hurt in his pride, as he put it, when his older married brother had inherited seventy per cent of the shares in the Patrucco family business while he had received a mere miserable thirty. Marcantonio had had the upper hand, made all the decisions, told him what to do. Had control. So the younger and disgruntled Domenico had just upped and left. America first stop, where, hot-headed and determined to show Marcantonio that he didn't need him or the olive plantations and the vineyards, he got into trouble over something to do with a parcel of land.

England next, to seek his fortune. What he had found was love. His Alice.

The only child of farming parents, Alice Mayhew had fallen head over heels with her handsome Italian suitor and after their marriage he'd helped out on the Shropshire farm; the income from the shares that had caused his permanent split from his brother had purchased more land, updated equipment and renovated the down-at-heel farmhouse.

However much he had despised the insulting smallness of his holding in the Italian business he had never sold those shares. And now, according to the healthy state of his bank balance, they were paying huge dividends.

'You didn't think family was important when you

upped and left Italy and broke off all contact,' Cat reminded him gently when she guessed by his continuing silence he had run out of things to say.

'That was pride. The pride of a man is stiff, unyielding.' He lifted his shoulders in a fatalistic shrug, but defended, 'I kept contact through our sister Silvana. She told me of Marcantonio's success in expanding the business, of the birth of his son, my nephew Astorre. Of my brother's death ten years after Astorre's marriage into a super-wealthy Roman family and the arrival of my great-nephew Aldo. Through her I know that Astorre has retired to Amalfi with his grand Roman wife and that Aldo now holds the business reins and has expanded into luxury holiday villas and apartments.'

Cat could almost feel sorry for him. A seventy-nine-year-old man indulging in pipedreams. She saw the relevance of that 'closing the circle' bit now. Sweep past resentments and quarrels aside, marry his granddaughter to his great-nephew and make everything right and whole again.

In his dreams!

'And through the photographs Silvana sent me—' a slow pause, a smile that might, if she were to be uncharitable, be described as sly '—I know that Aldo is a fine figure of Italian manhood—at thirty years of age he has a truly astute business brain and is the owner of a villa in Tuscany, a town house in Florence and an apartment in Portofino—*che bello*! You could do far worse! That I know all that is important to know about my lost family I explained to Aldo when I spoke to him on the phone a fortnight ago and suggested that a marriage between you two young things might be arranged to reunite the family.'

A beat of appalled silence. Cat felt her face colour hotly. 'You did *what*? I do not *believe* this!' Then the cool and welcome slide of common sense effectively stopped her exploding with outrage. 'And he quite rightly told you where to put your interfering ''suggestion''. Right?'

'Far from it. He accepted my invitation to come and meet you. To discuss the matter further. As I said, he has an astute brain. Which brings us to my shares.' He held out his cup and saucer. 'Would you?'

Rising, Cat poured his second cup of tea, her hands shaking. She would not let her temper rip. Her grandfather was seventy-nine years old; he was grieving for his Alice. His sister was also, sadly, gone. He couldn't make his peace with his older brother—he had died many years ago. He wanted to heal the family rift through his granddaughter and his great-nephew. She had to keep reminding herself of the facts to stop herself throttling him!

So she wouldn't storm out of here as every instinct urged her to. She really didn't want to upset him. Besides, no one on this earth could make her marry a man she didn't know, quite possibly wouldn't even like and certainly wouldn't love.

Reassured, she handed him his tea and asked, 'So when does this paragon arrive?'

'Any time now. I didn't tell you what I had in mind earlier. You would have suddenly expressed the wish to take a walking holiday in Scotland or go climbing in the Andes!'

Cat dipped her head, acknowledging his correct reading of her character. She recalled a note appended to one of her end-of-term reports. 'Caterina is stubborn and headstrong. She won't be led and she won't be pushed.'

Bolshie, in other words.

She preferred to think of herself as strong-minded. She knew what she wanted and that wasn't having to endure being looked over by some Italian big shot like a heifer at market!

'Why aren't you shouting at me, Caterina?'

The thread of amusement in his voice brought her attention back to her grandfather. She gave a slight, dismissive shrug and walked to the window to look out at the tail end of the afternoon. The days were shortening and the turning leaves of the damson tree mimicked the promise of hazy sunshine breaking through the warm and heavy early-autumn mist.

'The timing of Aldo's arrival is irrelevant. He is wasting his time coming here at all.' She turned back to face him, the russet colour of the heavy-duty smock she usually wore when she was working emphasising the burnished glow of her chestnut hair, making her skin look paler, her eyes a deeper emerald. She spread her long-fingered artist's hands expressively. 'I can't understand why he's bothering. The guy's obviously loaded and unless he looks like a cross between Quasimodo and a pot-bellied pig he could take his own pick of women.'

'As no doubt he has,' Domenico remarked drily. 'But when it comes to taking a wife there is much to be considered. Family honour demands that a man marries wisely and well and not merely because he has lustful desires for a particular pretty woman.'

'Your shares in his business,' Cat deduced in a flat voice. This Aldo creep was obviously the pits. Popular culture marked the Italian male as being passionate, hot-blooded and fiery but this distant relative of hers had to be anything but if he could contemplate, even for one moment, marrying a woman he had yet to meet for the sake of clawing back a parcel of shares.

Verifying that conclusion, Domenico dipped his head. 'My thirty-per-cent holding in his business, plus everything that is mine will one day come to you.' He stirred his tea reflectively. 'You are young, you are beautiful and when I am gone you will be all alone. If you were safely married to a man such as Aldo your future would be secure. You would be part of a family, cared for and pampered. I do not make this suggestion because I am crazy but because I love you and worry about your future.'

'There's no need,' Cat said gruffly, her throat thickening. On the one hand she wanted to give him a verbal lashing. He was like something out of the ark! In his outdated opinion women couldn't stand on their own feet; they needed a member of that superior race—a man—to look after them. And when he was no longer around to perform that duty he wanted to pass her over to someone he thought he could trust! He was living back in the nineteenth century—and, what was worse, an Italian nineteenth century!

On the other hand, she knew he loved her, cared about her, and that made her want to fling her arms around him and tell him she loved him, too.

She did neither. She said, relatively calmly, 'I'm a big girl; I can look after myself. And if we really must have to anticipate events—which is not what I want to do—then I have a business of my own, remember. I could sell those shares to invest in it,' she pointed out. 'I could buy more and better equipment, hire staff, open a proper high-street shop instead of trading from a craft centre. I have no intention of tying myself to a cold-fish business brain for the sake of a life of idle luxury!' She turned to the door, telling him, 'You'd better start thinking of how to apologise to the guy for bringing him over here on a wild-goose chase.'

'Wait.' Domenico's voice was smooth as cream. 'Marriage is by no means certain. Though I know Aldo wouldn't have agreed to this meeting if he hadn't thought the idea viable. And I warn you, if he does propose and you turn him down for no good reason but pigheadedness—going against my wishes and your own best interests—then the shares, every-thing I have, will go to him.'

For several long seconds Cat couldn't move. A heavy ache balled in her chest and her eyes flooded with tears. Gramps had said he loved her but he was quite happy to blackmail her. It hurt more than he would ever know.

The loss of her inheritance paled into insignificance. It would be tough, but she'd manage. When the time came she would have to find new living and working premises to rent, work all hours in order to keep her tiny business viable, and maybe not make it.

But that was nothing beside the knowledge that he was prepared to disinherit her if she didn't toe the line. He couldn't care for her at all, or not as much as he cared for what he called family honour.

When she could get her feet to move she walked out of the room and exactly one hour later she saw Aldo Patrucco arrive from the vantage point of her kitchen window above the cobbled stack yard.

He exited from the back of a dark saloon. He was tall, wearing a beautiful dark grey overcoat and a white silk scarf, and that was all she could see because the mist that had been hanging around all day had thickened in the autumn evening.

The uniformed chauffeur took a single leather suitcase from the boot and moments later drove away. So the big shot must have hired the package, Cat deduced as the main door was opened by Bonnie to admit the Italian.

Cat shuddered, her mouth clamped decisively shut.

Only ten minutes ago Bonnie had called from the bottom of the stairs that led up from her work-room, telling her that her grandfather expected her to take dinner with him and his guest. Eight o'clock sharp.

She could refuse to put in an appearance. Or she could turn up in her shabbiest work clothes, display disgraceful table manners and vile personal habits, and put the guy off the idea of having anything at all to do with her.

The latter idea was tempting but she had too much pride to let herself act with such immaturity. She would go. She would be dignified. Not speak until spoken to. And spend her time trying to calculate if the amount in her bank balance would fund the renting of new premises if her grandfather threw her out as soon as Aldo Patrucco had left England, his proposal of marriage—if he made it—rejected with the scorn it deserved.

CHAPTER ONE

MARRYING Aldo Patrucco had been the biggest mistake of her life, Cat told herself for the millionth time as she stood in front of the tall window at the top of the villa, staring out at the rolling Tuscan hills shimmering in the haze of afternoon heat.

The panoramic view might once have entranced her. But the gentle purple hills, silver olive groves and scattered ochre-coloured farmhouses, the ubiquitous punctuation marks of the cypress trees merely emphasised her isolation, her frustration and misery.

The villa—every luxury provided...well, that went without saying in a Patrucco residence—reputedly built for the Medici family way back in the middle ages, had been her prison for two long months, since shortly after her miscarriage back in June.

Apart from his twice-weekly dutiful phone calls she'd had no contact with Aldo; he'd used his excuse of 'Rest and Recuperation' to get her away from the house in Florence, out of his sight, masking his disappointment in her failure to carry his heir to full term with an unconvincing display of polite concern for her well-being.

Leaving him free to be with his mistress.

He was cold. Heartless. Unreachable. Except...

Except she'd once been so sure he hadn't been like that at all, that she could somehow reach his heart.

But he hadn't got a heart, had he? Just an efficient machine, like a calculator.

As it too often did, her mind slid back with humiliating ease to that fatal night when she'd first met him. Only eleven months ago but it seemed like a lifetime now.

Dinner at eight. True to her intention to grit her teeth and make an appearance, to present a dignified front, she'd dressed in the soberest garment she owned. A peacock-green crêpe shift that skimmed her generously curved body and left her arms bare. Her make-up discreet, her unmanageable hair somehow tamed, drawn back from her face and painstakingly secured with a black velvet bow at her nape.

'Caterina—' There'd been such a note of pride in her grandfather's voice as he'd risen from a leather club chair in the study as she'd walked into the room with her head high, but his introduction was lost on her as Aldo Patrucco got to his feet.

Over six feet of superbly dressed Italian male, a strong, harshly handsome face, his features shimmering out of focus because it was the look in those bitter-chocolate eyes that entrapped her.

She'd seen that look in men's eyes before and had uninterestedly ignored it. Her one and only short-lived affair with Josh, a fellow student, in her final year at college had fizzled out with no regret on either side, and since then she hadn't been remotely tempted.

But this hot, sultry branding held her as she'd never been held before, and her lips parted on a breathless gasp as his hard mouth curved in a slight, lazy smile just before he greeted her with easy Italian panache, his hands resting lightly on her shoulders, a light kiss on her forehead, another just above the corner of her mouth.

Just the softest brush of his lips against her skin, but it was enough to make her shake, make her breathless, disorientated.

'Ciao, Caterina.' His voice slid over her like warm dark honey. She mumbled something and turned away to hide the heat that suddenly flared over her face. She preferred to be called Cat—it sounded sharper, definite, more like the self she knew herself to be— but Caterina, on his lips, sounded like magic.

Charm, she told herself, making no attempt to join in the ensuing conversation, which was being conducted in part Italian, part English. He could turn charm on like a tap. Obviously. So why was she feeling hot and bothered, overpowered, when she had to know that the way he had looked at her, as if he wanted to bed her right here and now, was just the stock-in-trade of a man who knew what he wanted and how to get it? A man who was fully aware of his power over other people and used it.

The physical presence of the man filled the book-lined room with a dangerous sexual threat. A combination of a lean, powerful six-foot frame clothed in sheer Italian elegance, and that closely cropped black hair framing hard tanned features, that tough jawline and a mouth that could soften into a wicked, explicit promise whenever he looked her way made a tense, fluttery excitement curl in the pit of her stomach.

Cat rose with a sense of relief when Bonnie poked her head round the door to announce that dinner was ready, a relief that quickly turned into deep trepidation when Aldo rose to escort her, the palm of his long, lean hand hot against the small of her back, burning her. Burning her up with a sheet of wildfire that sizzled through her veins and made her feel lightheaded.

No other man had ever affected her this way. She'd sort of fallen into her brief affair with Josh because he fancied her, was easy on the eye, and had been amusing company. And it had seemed to her that she was the only girl in her peer group not in a relationship. But this feeling was entirely different. It was immediate, insistent. Shattering.

Seated opposite him, Cat didn't know where to put herself, and Bonnie's meal, beautifully cooked and presented as usual, was untouched on her plate. But the champagne Gramps had insisted on eventually loosened her tongue and Aldo's dark eyes locked on to her soft mouth as he murmured, 'You speak fluent Italian.'

'I was brought up on it—my grandparents insisted.' She drained her glass, feeling reckless, feeling more like herself. The situation was weird, like something out of an old and rather silly novel, but undoubtedly exciting. What woman wouldn't be feeling as if she were permanently plugged into a conduit for live electricity when face to face with such a breathtakingly sexy, brain-blowingly gorgeous male who was here with the express intent of looking her over, deciding whether she was suitable wife material?

'Caterina has always been made aware of her heritage,' Domenico put in with an undertow of satisfaction, like a breeder demonstrating the finer points of his bloodstock to a possible purchaser.

Far from experiencing all that earlier outrage, Cat giggled softly as she watched the bubbles rise in the crystal flute as Aldo helped her to yet more champagne. 'I have far more English blood in my veins than Italian,' she argued softly, feeling those bitter-chocolate eyes on her and secretly wallowing in the sensation of feeling more truly alive than she had ever done before.

Aldo leaned back in his chair, his eyes hooded now as they roamed from the crown of her glossy chestnut head, over her milky white skin and down to the lushly rounded breasts beneath the soft covering of fine fabric, the explicit shafts of golden light in the veiled depths making her blush as he murmured, 'With your colouring, your grace, you could be *Veneziana*, and I hear from Zio Domenico that your temperament is fiery, pure *Italiana*, with nothing of the phlegmatic English.'

'And could you cope with that, *signor*?' she dared, green eyes sparkling through a thick sweep of dark lashes as she thrust the agenda out into the open, wondering if such exposure would wrong-foot this supremely self-assured male, unprepared for and wantonly excited by his softly drawled comeback, the slow and decidedly rakish grin that made her pulse flutter.

'I am quite sure I could. With much pleasure.'

His purring, silken response filled her head with X-rated images. Married to him, enjoying him. His mouth on hers, giving her the heaven it had so far only promised, his hard, honed naked body covering hers, demanding, taking, possessing... It would be criminally easy to give him exactly what his eyes told her he wanted and then ask him for more!

She couldn't tear her eyes away from his; he mesmerised her, turned her blood to fire, filled her with aching need. And her breathing was going haywire, her pulse throbbing as Domenico rose to his feet, satisfaction in his voice after following their exchange as he announced softly, 'You must excuse me. I am an old man and retire early. Caterina, why don't you show Aldo where you work and give him coffee?'

Which was what she needed, yet didn't need at all. She wanted to be alone with him and yet the prospect scared her witless. She didn't trust herself around this man, she didn't trust herself at all and yet the prospect was heady, electrifying, disturbingly exciting.

Aldo stood and turned to speak to her grandfather, his voice low-pitched. Cat wasn't listening and she didn't look at him either. It wasn't safe.

Looking at him, drowning in that warm, honeyed voice short-circuited her brain. She needed to come down out of fantasy land and plant her feet firmly on the ground, put her brain in gear and tell him she knew exactly why he was here.

Tell him he didn't need to waste any more of his doubtlessly precious time looking her over because the idea of their marriage was a non-starter.

And yet...

Angrily, she squashed the treacherous beginnings of a mental veer in the opposite direction, the shafting thought that it would be much too easy to fall helplessly in love with this man, that marriage to him would be a challenge, exciting, endlessly rewarding.

Indulging in wild fantasies was alien to her, alien, unwanted and unnecessary. It was time she did something about it, put a stop to all this nonsense. Laying down her napkin, she, too, got to her feet and said stiltedly, 'Bonnie will bring coffee, *signor*; I'll ask her on my way out. So I'll say goodnight, too, Grandfather. I'm sure your guest has no desire to see a workshop.'

'I have every desire, Caterina.' The silken stroke of his voice made every muscle in her body tighten. His stress on that word 'desire' left her in no doubt that he wasn't referring to her work benches and tools. And the gleam in his eyes as he let them drift lazily over her taut body terrified her. Already she had a violently insane need to get closer, to loop her arms around those wide, immaculately clad shoulders and submit the soft, melting femininity of her body to his hard domination.

She had to be losing her mind! Resisting the impulse to cover her burning face with her shaking hands, Cat made a strenuous mental effort to pull herself together.

She was free, she was independent, she had her work and she loved it. She was passionate about everything she had, and had no intention of accepting a hand-picked husband, selected and presented in cold blood.

It was her misfortune that the man in question was sexier than any man had a right to be. What she was experiencing was lust, she reminded herself tartly. Just lust. All the more shattering because she'd been celibate for a long time, ever since she and Josh had broken up before the end of their final year at college.

Having been left with no other option, Cat led the way over the cobbled yard, picking her way carefully on the uneven surface. The security lights were on but she was used to striding around in flat shoes and jeans or flowing, colourful skirts, and the skirt of the dress she was wearing was narrow and tight and her heels, although restrainedly elegant, were too high.

She more than half expected him to slide an intimate hand around her waist on the pretext of steadying her slow and tottery progress but he did nothing of the sort. She didn't know whether to feel glad about that or strangely deprived. Whatever, her heart was beating so violently she was sure it would burst out of her chest.

As always, the double doors opened easily at her touch and as she depressed the light switch Aldo remarked coolly, 'You don't lock your premises?'

Cat shrugged slim shoulders. 'Sometimes. If I'm out for any length of time. Does it matter?' Which was her way of saying, Is it any of your business?

'It shows carelessness.'

Wow! His mood had changed quicker than she could bat an eyelash! Watching the lean grace of his beautifully clad body as he ignored her and walked further into the studio, the way his long hands slid carefully over the thin sheets of silver laid out on one of the work benches, she felt sick with disappointment.

Oh, grow up! she snapped at herself. She couldn't really want to fight a losing battle with him if he had brought that earlier covert seduction out into the open. Of course not. She should be deeply relieved that, away from her grandfather's watchful eyes, he had reverted to what he truly was—cold and calculating.

He held up the garnet ear droppers she had been working on earlier, switching on the desk lamp and turning them to the light, examining the moulded silver settings before laying them carefully down again and going to stand in front of the open sketch book displaying her designs for future projects.

'You have a certain talent.' He turned to her, his hands on the narrow span of his hips. And then he lifted his impressive shoulders in a dismissive shrug. 'Your grandfather tells me you sell your creations from a stall in a draughty, redundant church. You barely scrape a living.'

'Don't knock it!' Cat's eyes narrowed. How dared he dish out such a put-down? Her fingers curled into the palms of her hands, biting into the tender skin. Earlier she had wanted to kiss him; now she wanted to kill him! The effort of holding her temper in check made her words come out bitingly fast. 'Everyone has to start somewhere. We're not all lucky enough to be handed a ready-made thriving business empire at birth. One day I'll have my own shop premises, a hand-picked team of craftsmen and women—'

'When you get your hands on your inheritance?' he slid in with insulting silkiness.

Cat's face closed up. Had Gramps told him about her recklessly defensive message about selling those precious family shares to fund her own small business, thoughtlessly tossed out to stop him boring on about his wretched idea for an arranged marriage? Or had it been an astute guess?

Whatever, she had no intention of defending herself to this patronising monster. She didn't want to get her hands on her inheritance, as he had callously put it, because it would mean that her beloved Gramps was no longer around and she couldn't bear the thought of that.

Her green eyes glittering with emotion, she spiked out, 'Please leave. Now!'

'So soon?' The indolent tilt of one dark brow, his aura of sophisticated and total command, was probably meant to intimidate her. It might have done, had she let it. She didn't.

'Can't be soon enough! You know where the door is.'

Unnervingly, his dark eyes gleamed with amusement. 'I also know I'm not leaving until we've thoroughly discussed your grandfather's wishes. He is an old man, far from the country of his birth, estranged from his family. The least we can do is discuss the pros and cons of his suggestion. Even if we think it's mad. Over coffee. This way?'

His dark head dipped towards the steep flight of wooden stairs that led to her living quarters. Cat ignored him. She bit her tongue to stop herself hurling verbal abuse at him as he mounted the stairs, arrogant self-confidence in every movement of his strong, supple body, then launched after him, kicking off her shoes and hiking her narrow, restrictive skirt above her knees.

Did he, too, think her grandfather's scheme was crazy? Had he come all this way to humour a distant relative he had never met out of respect? Italians went a bundle on respect, didn't they?

But the question flew out of her head as he reached the apartment well ahead of her, despite her best efforts in the scampering department. The door opened directly into her living room. She had left a table lamp burning and the room just looked like comfortable chaos. But when he found the main light switch and depressed it the room looked like a squalid hovel.

And Aldo, standing in the middle of the muddle, was so beautifully groomed and immaculate. The contrast made her cheeks flame with embarrassment. The velvet bow that had held her hair in check fell off. She heard it hit the floor behind her just before the riotous chestnut tangle tumbled around her shoulders. And she was still holding her skirt above her knees. She dropped the hem immediately and said starkly, 'Coffee?' and picked her barefoot way through to the tiny kitchen, avoiding the piles of trade magazines and glossies, the pile of curtains she'd laundered but hadn't got around to re-hanging and the heap of work clothes she'd got out of before going through to shower and change earlier this evening.

When she was working, deeply engrossed in a new project, she forgot to be tidy, forgot everything. But no way would she explain or make excuses to this so obviously superior being, who probably had an army of servants to keep everything around him picture perfect plus one in reserve just to iron his shoelaces.

Thankfully, he didn't follow her to the kitchen to sneer at the empty baked-bean tin with the spoon still in it. There'd been nothing else for breakfast because she'd forgotten to shop and the Belfast sink was overflowing with unwashed dishes, but at least she did have decent coffee.

When she carried the tray through he had his back to her. He was studying the framed prints that broke the severity of the white-painted walls. Nudging aside a bowl of wilting roses, she set the tray down on the low table that fronted the burnt-orange-upholstered small sofa then stood very straight, dragging in a deep breath.

Time to get the show on the road. Throw Gramps's stupid idea straight out of play and get on with the rest of her life. The old man would be deeply disappointed, she knew that, and would probably carry through his threat to disinherit her, but she could handle that.

'So you think my grandfather's idea of an arranged marriage is mad,' she stated for starters, carefully keeping her voice level, non-confrontational as she waited for his robust confirmation of what he'd said earlier. And watched him turn, very slowly.

'Not necessarily.' His lean features betrayed nothing. 'It was idle supposition on my part—on your behalf. Do you really think I would have come this far if I'd thought the idea had no merit?' He strolled with an appallingly fluid grace to where she was standing. 'Shall I pour, or will you?'

The question didn't register. Cat's mouth ran dry, her lips parted. She gasped for air; she felt she was being suffocated. From his attitude since they'd taken leave of her grandfather she'd drawn the conclusion that he'd been humouring the old man, had as little intention as she did of entering into an arranged marriage. Now it seemed the game was back on. It was a deeply terrifying prospect.

Though why that should be she couldn't work out. No one could force her to marry anyone!

'Your silence tells me you don't care either way. About who should pour the coffee.' A strange satisfaction threaded through his voice and curved his lips. Cat's eyes went very wide as they locked on to that sinfully sexy mouth. Her own lips felt suddenly desperately needy and she was hot, much too hot; she could spontaneously combust at any moment!

The silence was stinging; it gathered her up and enclosed her with him, very tightly, and there was no escape. Her flurried gasp of relief was completely involuntary when he finally broke the awful tension and turned to pour the coffee.

Taking his own cup, he angled his lean body into one corner of the sofa, long legs stretched out in front of him, the sleek fabric caressing the taut muscles of his thighs like the touch of a lover.

Cat gulped thickly. Her thoughts were so wicked! She had to blank them, and when he glanced at the vacant space beside him and invited softly, 'Shall we talk?' she shied away, wrapping her arms around her trembling body, and had to force herself to say, 'There's nothing to talk about,' because the temptation to join him, sit intimately close, was enormous.

And very, very dangerous!

'No? No opinions?' he queried softly, his honeyed tone giving her goose bumps. The look in his eyes as they fastened on her hectically coloured face made her stop breathing. 'Then I'll give you mine, shall I?'

Cat forced herself to move, to give a slight, careless shrug before she picked her way over to a vaguely throne-like chair she'd picked up one Sunday afternoon at a car-boot sale. It's slightly vulgar ostentation had amused her but it was supremely uncomfortable.

Aldo was watching her, his eyes hooded, looking smoky. Seated, Cat kept her eyes firmly on her bare toes. He could spout opinions all night but that didn't mean she needed take the slightest notice of them.

But her heart was beating uncomfortably fast as he raised his arms and laced his hands behind his head and told her, 'I have nothing against arranged marriages, all things being equal. Up until now I've been too busy to consider marrying. I confess to never having been in love, and unlike most of my compatriots,' he added drily, 'I consider the condition to be vastly overrated. It dresses the basic human need to procreate in romantic flummery.'

Cat's eyes shot up from the anodyne contemplation of her toes to lock with his. 'So you don't believe in love,' she challenged. Her eyes gleamed. 'Bully for you! I bet you a dime to a king's ransom the right woman could teach you differently!'

Brilliant dark eyes sparked with pinpricks of golden light at her husky outburst but his voice was cool when he continued as if she hadn't spoken, 'As far as I'm concerned, marriage is a serious matter. An heir is necessary. Any wife I choose would have to be intelligent, good to look at, have her feet firmly on the ground—no girlish claims to be madly in love with me because such emotional demands would merely make life difficult. Besides all this, I would need her to bring something of substance to the marriage. Family honour as well as sound financial sense demands that much.' He brought his hands down, his beautifully cut jacket settling back against his upper body with exquisite, unruffled elegance. 'I think you qualify on all counts.'

'Especially Grandfather's shares,' she said on a dry snap. 'Couldn't you offer to buy them off him—twist his arm or something? You could save yourself a whole heap of trouble.' If what he'd been saying was supposed to be a proposal then it was the coldest, most calculating one any woman was ever likely to hear. It deserved her utmost contempt. It showed in the green glitter of her eyes, in the tight downturn of her generous mouth.

Water off a duck's back as far as Aldo was concerned, apparently. He expanded his argument fluidly. 'Perhaps Domenico would agree to sell; perhaps not. But I have no intention of going down that road. Why should I when I can kill three birds with one stone? One,' he ticked off on his long, tanned fingers, 'I secure those possibly rogue shares for the family, where they belong. Two, I get a beautiful and intelligent wife, and three, I get an heir. And as far as you're concerned, you get a pampered lifestyle, more financial security than you've ever dreamed of—'

'I don't need it!' Distraught, Cat shot to her feet, her breasts heaving. Listening to this man—this...this sex-on-legs—talking of marriage as if it were a cold business arrangement was the last thing she wanted. 'I don't want your empty wealthy lifestyle—I want my own life, warts and all. I'm a big girl, *signor*; I can stand on my own feet, or hadn't you noticed?'

'Oh, I noticed,' he countered, smooth as cream. He rose to his feet and sauntered towards her and she gritted her teeth. He had too much style. He was too much altogether. And this close she could see those intriguing golden lights deep within his eyes, breathe in the elusive male scent of him, and her mouth fell open on a trembling gasp as he whispered seductively, 'You truly are a big girl.' His eyes slid down and lingered on her breasts, which annoyingly responded to this devastating no-touching slide of seduction. 'But only, I assure you, in all the most enticing places.'

'Don't!' Cat's command came out on a tortured whisper. When he turned on the sex, flooded his voice with it, she went to pieces.

He was lethal!

'Why not? It's a bonus.' Another movement, a step closer.

His black eyes looked drugged as he lifted them slowly from her shamelessly peaking breasts and fastened them on her softly trembling mouth as she muttered defensively, 'I don't know what you're talking about!'

'Yes, you do.'

The tension was making her shake, making the fine

hairs on the back of her neck stand to attention. The sheer sexual power of the man overwhelmed her. She wanted to fight it but didn't know how.

'A wife who would excite me in bed would be a bonus. Yes?' The soft huskiness of his voice was an unbearable intimacy; it made the blood pound in her ears and her whole body burn. He was much too close. She stared at him wildly. She had to put more space between them. At any moment she could find herself grabbing him, pulling his head down to discover if the promise of that so sensual mouth was capable of delivery.

Cat tried to move but her legs were so weak she could only sway. Aldo's hand slid to her shoulder to steady her and an electric storm fizzled through every cell in her body and her eyelids closed helplessly as his knowing fingers stroked the heated skin of her naked shoulder before it brushed with wicked intimacy over the tingling peaks of her aching breasts.

'And you would be excited, too. We would be dynamite together. I feel it and so do you. Yes?' His hands curved over her hips as he gently tugged the span of her against the hardness of him and the shattering excitement that flooded her produced a ragged sound, halfway between a gasp and a moan. As he lowered his sleek dark head to stifle the sound at source, her arms snaked around his neck, and her last coherent, triumphant thought as he plundered her avidly responsive mouth was a repetition of what she'd said to him earlier—I bet you a dime to a king's ransom the right woman could teach you differently!

The sounds of a muted commotion in the courtyard far below brought Cat out of her thoughts of the past. Blinking the film of moisture from her eyes, she peered down. At the sight of Aldo's silver Ferrari her heart leapt and twisted like a landed fish then dropped with heavy lifelessness to the soles of her bare feet as he exited, and walked round to the passenger side to hand out his mistress.

Three members of staff were milling around in excited welcome at their beloved master's unexpected arrival. Cat willed him to look up to where she was standing, to appear remotely interested in her whereabouts. But he didn't glance towards the villa. His attention was all for Iolanda Cardinale, who was clinging to his arm, her sleek, elegantly clothed body leaning possessively into his, her ripe lips parted with sultry promise.

Fighting nausea, Cat forced herself to creep down the spiral staircase to her suite of rooms. She was going to have to act her socks off if she was going to be able to pretend she could accept the situation.

Pride wouldn't allow her to let either of them see how desperate she was. Love and sexual fidelity hadn't been part of the bargain on his part, had it?

As her English grandmother would have said, 'You've made your bed, girl. Now you must lie on it.'

CHAPTER TWO

REACHING her rooms and closing the bedroom door behind her, Cat leaned back weakly against the carved wood. She was going to have to face him. Them.

Why had he chosen to arrive unannounced? Why had he brought Iolanda Cardinale with him?

Because he was cruel.

Or simply because this sort of thing went on in the elevated circles in which he moved and he didn't consider it to be even slightly unusual?

And how long were they staying? Overnight? Would he share this room with her?

Grimly, she thought not. He hadn't bothered to visit during her exile and he hadn't so much as touched her since she'd told him—dewy-eyed and stupid with love for him—of the confirmation of her pregnancy.

Besides, he wouldn't even think about sharing her bed when he had his mistress draped all over him!

On that draining thought she levered herself tiredly away from the door and walked further into the lovely room. Apart from the gilded four-poster bed the furnishings and decorations were a dreamy medley of white and creams, gauzy drapes fluttering at the tall windows that looked out over the sun-drenched landscape, over the silver olive groves and purple hills.

She would have to prepare herself, put on the cam-ouflage of warpaint and chic designer armour, and as if on cue Rosa came bouncing in after a decidedly hysterical rap on the door.

'*Il padrone* has arrived! So unexpected—every-one's running round in circles! Did you know? Why didn't you tell us to make ready? Come, I will help you dress, make yourself beautiful for him!'

Cat forced a thin smile. Rosa, assigned as her per-sonal maid on her arrival here two months ago, had become her dresser, her nanny, her arbiter of correct behaviour and her friend. Unlike the other members of staff Rosa wasn't painfully deferential and she didn't whisper behind her hands when she thought she was out of earshot. And no, Aldo hadn't said anything about finally deigning to visit her the last time he'd phoned her.

'You have already bathed?' Rosa didn't wait for an answer, bustling towards the huge hanging cupboard that almost filled one wall, tutting disapprovingly as her eyes fell on the untouched breakfast tray. 'You must eat, *signora*. You lose too much weight already.' She pulled out one of the fitted drawers and handed Cat her selection of underwear, filmy, lacy pale cream briefs and bra, her kind eyes softening. 'I understand how you feel about losing your baby; it was a terrible thing to happen, but an accident of nature and nothing to blame yourself for. There will be other babies for you.'

Nothing to blame herself for? She knew differently.

Removing her wrap and dressing in the understated chic of the smoky-grey sleeveless shirt-shift Rosa had put out for her, Cat shivered as the cool silk whispered against her body. She'd been assured at the private clinic where she'd been taken on that dreadful night that the early miscarriage had been nature's way of coping when everything was not as it should be.

She had said nothing to oppose the well-meaning platitudes but she'd known that if she hadn't been so tense and anxious she wouldn't have lost her baby.

Aldo had politely and coolly distanced himself from her when he'd heard of the coming baby. Overjoyed at the news of her pregnancy, of course, and very solicitous.

Too solicitous, she'd felt smothered. Her eager explorations of the beautiful old city with her husband as her attentive guide had been firmly vetoed and he'd given orders to his staff at their Florence home that she was to rest, take a little gentle exercise in the cool of the day with Beppe, an ancient retainer who could walk no faster than a snail, as her companion.

And Aldo himself had been away more often than he'd been at home, catching up on the business responsibilities he'd neglected since their marriage, or so he'd said, and worst of all moving out to another bedroom.

'You are carrying my child,' he told her gently when she'd protested. 'If I share your bed I will make love to you; I will not be able to help myself. And our loving is fierce, truly passionate. Yes? I will do nothing to harm you or the tiny life you carry.'

In view of the way he'd ordered everyone to treat her as if she were made from the finest of brittle spun glass, she might have believed him. She might have lovingly teased him about being over-protective if Iolanda Cardinale hadn't dripped all that poison into her ears.

She'd refused to believe a word of what the hateful woman had said but the change in Aldo's attitude towards her when he'd learned of her pregnancy had forced her to acknowledge that Iolanda could have been telling the truth. Her tortured thoughts, her aching anxiety had to be responsible for that miscarriage.

Dutifully seating herself in front of the long mirror in its ornate gilded frame, she watched Rosa working on her hair, brushing it back from her face and securing it neatly in a French pleat.

It had been the first grand dinner party Aldo had thrown on their return from honeymoon, she remembered with a stab of the usual pain. Mainly for the benefit of business associates and friends who hadn't been able to attend the wedding and be introduced to his new bride at the lavish reception.

Iolanda, as Aldo's executive PA, had been there, oozing the understated chic Italians were so good at. Her svelte, cool loveliness had made Cat feel gaudy and overdressed in her swirly skirted, bootlace-strapped confection in her favourite shade of vibrant scarlet.

Wandering out onto the terrace to catch a breath of the cool evening air, Iolanda had joined her. As the only unpartnered guest at the gathering Cat had made a point of drawing Iolanda into the conversation around the dinner table so she wouldn't feel left out. So her smile was wide as she acknowledged the other woman.

'I would like to talk to you,' Iolanda said.

'That's nice! It's getting rather stuffy inside, isn't it?' Perhaps, being on her own, the other woman was feeling a bit out of things now that dinner was over and the guests circulating, forming chattering groups. 'Shall we find somewhere to sit? There are seats—'

'No.' The other woman cut across her, a note of impatience in her drawl. 'This will only take moments. In view of the situation I thought we ought to be properly introduced.'

'I thought we had been.' Cat smiled, puzzled, wondering if she'd missed something. Iolanda shook her head slowly, her smooth, raven-dark hair gleaming in the overflow of light from the main salon, her answering smile slight, tight and superior.

'Not really. You are Aldo's wife. I am Aldo's mistress. Ordinarily, we would of course know of each other's existence but we would not meet. Discretion in such matters is important—that is understood. But as Aldo and I work so closely together our occasional meetings cannot be avoided. I thought we should understand our positions. Suspicions and speculations only make life uncomfortable, as I'm sure you would grow to learn when you have done your duty and given him an heir and he begins to spend more time away from you than with you and you wonder why.'

Again that hateful, superior little smile that left Cat speechless with a mixture of rage and disbelief at what she was hearing. 'That being said, I would strongly advise you against making a fuss about a situation which a man in Aldo's position regards as being absolutely normal. An hysterical fuss would only serve to estrange him from you entirely and do you no good at all.'

'There—all done.' Rosa stepped back, surveying the neat outcome of her ministrations with satisfaction. 'I'll leave you to do your make-up. Be sure you cover up those dark circles round your eyes and put some colour on your cheeks!'

Cat watched her reflection with no enthusiasm at all. She no longer looked like herself. Her exuberant hair had been flattened and tamed, her mouth drooped and her eyes looked haunted.

She'd been stunned, knocked speechless by what Iolanda had said, but she hadn't believed a word of it. She'd refused to let herself believe it. The woman was obviously a raving idiot! Iolanda wanted Aldo for herself and was out to make mischief.

Having every intention of telling Aldo of his assistant's crazed lies, she'd changed her mind when as soon as the last guest had departed he'd swept her up in his arms and carried her up the sweeping staircase.

'I don't know how I've managed to keep my hands

off you!' he breathed rawly. 'All evening long I've wanted to rip your clothes off, bury myself inside you and make endless, endless love to you!'

And he'd done just that, she remembered with a fierce stab of pain. He'd ripped the scarlet dress right from the dipping neckline to the swirly-flirty hem, the wild, fiery passion of his lovemaking making a complete nonsense of Iolanda's wicked lies. Mentioning what the other woman had said would be a mistake. He would think she was only asking for reassurance, didn't trust him, and would resent it. Far more sensible to dismiss the distasteful episode from her mind.

But later, listening to the soft sound of his regular breathing, the first uncomfortable pinpricks of doubt had crept in as she'd wondered why the only real closeness they ever achieved was between the sheets, and why he always turned his back on her and immediately fell asleep after making love with her.

Having sex, she tiredly corrected. The only time he'd mentioned the word love had been when he'd confessed that he didn't believe in the condition. And had he only completely ruined her dress because he'd thought that was all the gaudy thing was fit for? Would he have treated Iolanda's elegant, wildly expensive black sheath with the same total lack of respect?

Turning on her side, she'd watched the first light of dawn filter through the partly closed window blinds. Perhaps there was a useful lesson she could learn. When in Rome, etc...

And so she'd set about turning herself into the type of woman Aldo would most respect and admire. If she couldn't have his love she could at least do her best to earn his respect.

Her still vibrant enthusiasm for every new project she took on board had ensured that her clothes were now the last word in unmistakable, understated Italian chic, her unmanageable mane of chestnut hair shortened and skillfully layered, *'Molto elegante!'* her horrendously expensive hairdresser had assured her, and she always wore spindly high heels to make sure her free-swinging stride was a thing of the past.

But her rapid transformation hadn't made a scrap of difference. He'd remained almost painfully polite and considerate, but distant. His eyes never smiled into hers, reminding her of shared intimacies the way lovers did; he never touched her except in bed.

When her pregnancy had been confirmed, her by then rapidly dwindling hope that things could be different between them soared high. That they had changed but not in the way she had wanted was something she hadn't foreseen, not in her worst nightmares.

Iolanda's words had come back to haunt her. 'You'll understand when you've done your duty and given him an heir and he starts to spend more time away from you than with you.' She hadn't given him an heir, she'd lost the precious baby she'd been longing for, but the signs had been there for anyone to see. As soon as he'd known of her pregnancy he'd wanted little more to do with her, his only concern the well-being of the child she was carrying.

Her stomach churning sickeningly at the memories that seemed to confirm everything that venomous woman had told her, Cat stood up from the dressing table, smoothing the silk of her dress over hips which were not as snake-like as Iolanda's, but getting there. Rosa was right—since she'd been banished after her miscarriage she had lost a lot of weight.

Facing her husband and his mistress with some semblance of dignity was the only thing she must make herself concentrate on right now, she decided with a welcome resurgence of the determination that had been absent for a long time.

But it drained away the moment the bedroom door swung open, revealing Aldo. He had the same unnerving impact on her as he'd had the very first time she'd set eyes on him. He took her breath away.

His dark business suit fitted his lean body to perfection and the crisp white shirt emphasised the bronzed skin of his austerely beautiful features. Cat veiled her eyes quickly. He was so unfairly gorgeous she couldn't bear to look at him.

'Caterina...' His voice was harsh; he had never directed that tone towards her before. His politeness had been the hallmark of their relationship.

Her puzzled eyes flickered upwards and met the glittering darkness of his. There were lines of strain on his face. She'd never noticed them before. 'You came here to recuperate, to regain your strength,' he condemned. 'What have you been doing to yourself?'

The heavy thumping of her heart quietened, subdued and regulated by an unexpected layer of heavy ice. How dared he criticise her, look at her as if her appearance offended him? She'd spent time and effort turning her exuberant self into what she'd hoped he'd appreciate—a model of Italian chic. And so what if she'd lost weight? Iolanda didn't exactly billow, did she? Or did fashion decree that Italian mistresses look like stick insects while Italian wives bulge comfortably in all directions?

Glacially, she held his darkly frowning eyes and intoned coldly, 'Since you haven't bothered to come and see what I've been "doing to myself",' she parodied his condemnatory tone, 'I'll tell you. Grieving,' she stressed tightly and inwardly flinched as lines of pain bracketed his stern mouth as her lashing remarks hit home.

'For our baby,' Aldo conceded with a softness that made her heart stand still. He took a step towards her. Cat retreated by a few rapid paces. If he belatedly remembered his abandoned husbandly role and tried to fold her in his arms to comfort her she would, quite simply, go to pieces and embarrass herself, and him, by blurting out all the sources of her present misery.

Turning back to the dressing table, she made a pretence of checking her appearance in the gilded mirror, replying, 'What else?'

She could have added, For the death of our marriage, for the loss of all hope that you'll ever learn to love me, but held her tongue because, to be fair to him, love hadn't been part of the bargain, just silly wishful thinking on her part.

But a mistress hadn't been part of the bargain either, she reflected trenchantly, and asked him brittly, 'Shall we go down? Had you let me know to expect you I'd have been waiting to greet you and your companion.' She swung towards the door, aware of his dark eyes boring into her back. 'What have you done with her, by the way?'

Aldo caught up with her as she opened the door, a lean, tanned hand snaking out to fasten disconcertingly on her shoulder. Desperately, Cat tried to control her weak body's electric reaction to his touch, to the effect of those bitter-chocolate eyes scorching into her own.

She dug her fingernails into the palms of her hands, using the resultant sharp sting of pain as an antidote to the overwhelming need to reach up her hands to touch that harshly handsome face, to beg him to open his heart to her, to love her, and only her.

But she wasn't so far sunk in physical and emotional weakness to let herself make such a fool of herself, was she? Some remnant of the old Cat surfaced from where it had been hiding and allowed her to meet those searching eyes with a flash of chilly disdain, and if Aldo had intended to say something then he obviously thought better of it, dropped his hand and made an after-you gesture towards the corridor outside her door.

Wordlessly, Cat preceded him, her back ramrod stiff, the only sounds that of their footsteps on the polished boarded floors, on the smooth stone steps of the wide staircase. There was so much to say, and yet nothing worth saying. Accusing him of neglect, of having a mistress, ranting and raving, would get her precisely nowhere. It would be water off a duck's back. He would simply give that insultingly insouciant shrug of his and continue doing exactly what he wanted.

With a hand on the small of her back, he guided her into a small sitting room at the rear of the villa, overlooking the beautifully tended gardens. Her entire system went into spasm. She didn't want him touching her. The resulting electric charge, the meltdown of her bones would remind her of the way things had been in the darkness of the night when he'd made love to her as if she were the only woman in the world for him.

She didn't want reminding, she wanted to forget. She jerked away, stepping sideways, and Aldo said, 'You worry me, Caterina. Your doctor assured me you were making steady progress.'

'So you bothered to check up?' Good, just enough scorn to bring his black brows together.

'Naturally. Every week, after his visit to you. You are my wife; of course I was concerned.'

'But not concerned enough to visit me yourself, to

stay with me.' The accusation came out smoothly, as if it wasn't really important to her. She had her pride and she was clinging on to it just as hard as she could. Let go of it and she'd start shouting and screaming at him and end up crying like a baby. To hide the sudden pulse of moisture in her eyes she walked to one of the windows and stared out, her vision blurred.

But her cool, almost uninterested words must have touched a nerve because she felt him moving closer, nearer to where she was standing, and heard him say gruffly, 'Ah, yes, I see. But I am with you now; everything has been put in order—'

What had been put in order was something she was destined not to know because the door opened and Iolanda trilled, 'Oh, I feel so much better! Please tell me I look better!'

'Much,' Cat heard Aldo say drily. She turned reluctantly, making her face expressionless. Iolanda was doing the classic exhibitionist's twirl, her slender arms outstretched. Her hair fell down her back like a waterfall of jet and she was wearing palazzo pants in a soft green chiffony fabric and a matching skimpy tunic top. Cat could see her nipples through the filmy fabric.

Coming to rest, the other woman sank gracefully onto a cream silk-covered sofa, her scarlet lips pouting. 'I hope you don't mind, but I asked one of the servants to take my luggage to a spare room. I needed more than a quick freshen-up. I had a divine shower and changed into fresh clothes—I was so hot and sticky after that long drive. Do tell me I have not abused your hospitality!'

'Of course not. I should have thought of it myself; it is I who should apologise.'

Aldo spoke with smooth urbanity but Cat knew from the rigid line of his shoulders, the firm set of his sensual mouth, that he was far from pleased. In his rarefied world wives and mistresses were kept in separate boxes, each satisfying different needs, never meeting each other and making life uncomfortable for him; that was the way the game was played.

Perversely, Iolanda's discomforting performance gave Cat a stab of bitter-sweet pleasure. Serve him right! And she could have applauded when the other woman leaned further back into the soft cushions and draped an arm along the back of the sofa, ensuring that her skimpy top rode up to display a couple of inches of taut, smooth-skinned midriff, her black eyes smouldering at him. Instead she asked coolly, 'May I offer you coffee, *signorina*?'

Dead silence, then a breathy little gasp coming from Iolanda. She shot an apologetic glance at Aldo between thick lashes. '*Signora*—I hadn't noticed you. What must you think of me?'

That you're a clever, dissembling little cow, Cat thought with uncharacteristic viciousness. Pretending you hadn't noticed me while confirming your position in my husband's life!

Or had she really been invisible with her pale, wan face and her melt-into-the-background smoky-grey dress? The thought produced a stab of hot anger. Before her ill-fated marriage she had been vibrant, outgoing, her flamboyant appearance drawing unwanted yet ego-boosting wolf-whistles when she walked down the street from the car park to the craft centre.

'Coffee?' Cat reiterated, feeling Aldo's brooding eyes on her and ignoring him.

'Oh, please—don't go to any trouble on my account. You should be resting, not trying to look after me,' Iolanda objected prettily. 'Aldo can do that in recompense for all the hard work I've put in for the company—you're obviously still unwell.'

Cat found a chair and sat on it. Miss Butterwouldn't-melt wasn't going to get rid of her so easily. And went hot with temper when after a barely discernible shrug Iolanda turned her now limpid eyes to Aldo. 'I think we deserve champagne, don't you? To celebrate our wonderful—successes?'

Directing a sweet smile towards Cat, she elaborated, 'You probably don't know much about your husband's business but we've been simply everywhere! Checking on all ends—grain, olives, grapes... you name it, we've checked it! I have been slavedriven! But it's been such fun, especially the acquisition of an almost intact castle on Sicily. It is run as an hotel, a shabby one. Such a pity! But in our hands it will be transformed into superb luxury holiday apartments. That was the best time.'

She gave a dreamy sigh. Her eyes were modestly

downcast but her smile was feline. 'We have been living in each other's pockets, travelling the length and breadth of the country for nearly two months, and now I am exhausted. I am so thankful I have the whole weekend before I need show my face in the Florence office.'

'I'm sure,' Cat responded drily, noting the frown line between Aldo's eyes as he turned and stalked out of the room, presumably to ask someone to put the champagne his mistress had demanded on ice.

Aldo Patrucco was definitely displeased!

The way Iolanda had flaunted herself, glanced at him with those come-bed-me eyes in front of his spare-wheel wife had annoyed him. It simply wasn't done in the sophisticated circles he moved in. The fact that she was now trying to make amends by turning all her attention on the wife wasn't cutting much ice, apparently.

Cat felt cold all over and then very hot. She wanted to take Iolanda by the scruff of her neck and throw her out. Her fingers curled into the palms of her hands as she fought to get her emotions under control. It was time she started fighting back. She wasn't a wimp and should stop behaving like one.

Aldo had only married her to get his hands on those wretched shares and she'd been one huge fool to think she could teach him to love her. But she was his wife—for the time being, she decided bitterly—and she deserved some respect. That he had brought his mistress here, to what was her home, or one of them, showed he had none.

It was time to forget she was stupid enough to love him and fight him as well!

She didn't know how, but she'd think of something!

'You are displeasing my husband.' Cat took the first battle to Iolanda, mentally and finally accepting that Iolanda had been telling the truth when she'd almost casually mentioned her mistress status. If she'd had any doubts before they'd gone now. Instead of being with her, comforting her over the loss of their baby, he had been with his mistress. 'Your attitude, the way you're dressed. I imagine he would expect you to know your place and behave, in my presence, like a mere employee. You are upsetting the status quo, jumping out of your box. Aren't you afraid he'll give you your marching orders? If you're not then perhaps you should be.'

If she'd been expecting embarrassment or fury Cat got neither. Iolanda merely hid a tiny yawn behind her long fingers, remarking, 'Oh, I don't think so. He finds me too irresistible—always has. Marriage was out of the question; I have nothing apart from what I earn and we all know why he did his duty and married you—my position in the company made it ridiculously easy to find that out. It's me he wants—oh, he'll make a show of wanting you, he'll shut his eyes, have sex, and think of his heir—and as for the way I'm dressed, Aldo will understand I need to be cool.

It is so very hot and we have been driving since dawn. We broke our journey by an overnight stay in Rome. It was more perfect than you can imagine...' She broke off as Aldo re-entered the room, and imparted brightly and untruthfully, 'I was just telling Signora Patrucco of a wonderful beautician I have heard of in Florence—apparently, she can work wonders, especially with women who have been dragged low by illness. I think the *signora* deserves such a tonic. I will be happy to find the telephone number for you.'

Thankfully, Cat was saved the indignity of leaping up and slapping the hateful creature by the arrival of the housekeeper with a tray of coffee. She blinked rapidly to dispel the red mist of rage as Iolanda rose gracefully to her feet.

'I will pour, shall I?' She addressed her limpid remark to Aldo, who regarded her unsmilingly from his vastly superior height. 'The *signora* must not exert herself.'

If she was disappointed by the non-appearance of the champagne she had as good as demanded, she certainly didn't show it as she dispensed coffee as if she were mistress of all she surveyed.

And when Aldo, pacing the room, his coffee-cup ignored, glanced at the slim gold watch on his wrist, Iolanda said demurely with a sly sideways glance at Cat, 'Aldo, I know you said you would have one of your staff drive me back to Florence after lunch, but would you reconsider?' She let her fabulous lashes droop. 'If it's not too much trouble, could I spend the night? I wasn't joking when I said I'm exhausted and we could spend the evening going over the facts and figures and making sure I've got everything right. I wouldn't want to make a mistake.'

She was making a huge one right now, Cat noted with dour satisfaction. Aldo's shoulders had gone rigid, and one dark brow elevated warningly. Iolanda might be his mistress, his irresistible mistress, but she was clearly stepping over the demarcation line. She was embarrassing him and he wouldn't want her under the same roof when he went to his wife's room, had sex for Italy, and tried to sire an heir in the place of the one she had lost.

Leaping in smoothly before he could veto the suggestion, Cat stuck a big false smile on her face and gushed, 'But of course you must stay. For as long as you like. I'll instruct the housekeeper.' And swept from the room, sensing Aldo's frowning eyes upon the suddenly vulnerable-feeling back of her head, and went to find the housekeeper, her mouth grim and tight.

If her intervention had put him on the spot, made him uncomfortable, then that meant she was at last fighting back. He deserved to feel uncomfortable. And if he read his precious mistress the Riot Act and asked her what she thought she was playing at then she, Cat, would have won the moral high ground!

But, instead of giving her satisfaction, the thought left her feeling decidedly sick.

CHAPTER THREE

'CATERINA...'

Aldo emerged from the shadows just as Cat was approaching her bedroom door. He must have followed her immediately, using the main staircase to her tower rooms. Her stomach plunged to the soles of her shoes. She'd stated her need for an early night and left him and Iolanda on the terrace as Maria, the housekeeper, had brought through the after-dinner coffee. She'd thought she'd handled her exit neatly, but apparently not.

His crisp white shirt was open at the neck and she could see a pulse beating rapidly at the base of his tanned throat. He skimmed her a veiled glance, his dark eyes narrowed and unreadable, and Cat's heart jumped. He looked so incredibly sexy, and the warm, clean scent of him swamped her with erotic memories, achingly insistent memories of the passion of their nights when she'd foolishly believed that he was beginning to really care for her.

'What is it?' she asked thinly as he reached forward to open the bedroom door, his hand brushing against hers, making her flinch away from the tingling contact. Heat sizzled between them and the tight, spiralling shaft deep inside her was naked, raw desire. And that was a definite no-no; she had to fight it.

His irresistible sexuality had trapped her right from their first meeting, overwhelming her, changing her from an independent free spirit to a mass of rioting hormones, willing to do anything, be anything for the paradisical pleasures of the marital bed. It wasn't going to happen again—as far as she was concerned their marriage was as good as over.

She entered the room, her spine ramrod straight. The lamps were already lit, the sheets turned back on the four-poster bed, and Rosa had laid out a fresh oyster satin nightdress and wrap.

What little colour she did have drained from her tense features as he followed her and closed the door behind him. Her whole body was reacting to the mere presence of his, her flesh quivering, her blood racing. She didn't know how to counteract it. She adored him but he had broken her heart. She didn't want the unfaithful swine near her!

Tearing her eyes from the suddenly frowning concentration of his, she bit out with a snappish lack of politeness, 'What do you want?'

'To be alone with my wife.' A small smile that lingered on his incredibly sexy mouth, a minimal shrug of those elegant shoulders, an inquisitorial upwards tilt of one dark brow. Cat drew in a ragged breath.

So he remembered he had one, did he? Because he'd checked with Dottore Raffacani and been given the go-ahead? Iolanda's vile prediction was coming true. He would have sex with her, shut his eyes and think of an heir.

Rage beat at her temples but Cat knew she had to stay cool. If she allowed herself to get emotional he'd take advantage, move in for the kill. Arching one brow, she commented drily, 'So you finally remembered my existence. It took you long enough—two months by my reckoning.'

The infuriating smile that again curved his beautiful mouth was a mixture of satisfaction and patronising amusement, Cat noted with a savage punch of blistering fury. Man-like, he thought she was sulking because she was feeling neglected and one kind word from him, one touch, would have her melting in his arms, pathetically eager to help him along in his efforts to do his duty and get her pregnant again.

Well, she wasn't sulking and her days of melting were well and truly over and she wanted to strangle him. And boil him in oil as a finishing touch as he stepped closer, his voice a husky murmur.

'*Cara*—I admit my absence was regrettable, but it really was necessary if—'

'I'm sure it was,' she cut right across him, feeling her face go tight with suppressed rage. 'Business, was it? And talking of your so-called business, you are neglecting your guest. I'm sure she's finished her coffee—'

'*Your* guest, *cara*.' It was his turn to cut her off in mid-flow as he reached for her in one smooth, unexpected movement, his hands resting lightly on her hips. 'It was you who pressed her to stay on, remember? I had arranged for her to be driven back to her home. I wanted rid of her.'

The heat of his hands, the gentle yet insistent pressure of his long fingers, the snare of his dark, stunning eyes combined to swamp her with a crashing wave of unwanted physical excitement. A shiver rocketed down her spine and all the way back up again, and her efforts to fight the effect his slightest touch had always had on her made every muscle in her body tense.

'I wanted to be alone with you, but instead Iolanda's been playing gooseberry. Of course,' he defended, making Cat cynically decide that perhaps he did have a conscience over his two-timing behaviour, at least as far as Iolanda was concerned, 'she won't have realised that. She's brilliant at what she does but she can be insensitive. She says and does things without thinking; she doesn't mean any harm.'

The way a viper means no harm when it sinks its venomous fangs into your flesh! And exactly where did her 'brilliance' lie? In her work or between the sheets?

Silly question!

And he'd obviously been referring to Iolanda's sugary-sweet suggestion that his wife visit a beautician, sit down before she fell down—all that stuff. He wouldn't want the women in his life tearing each other's hair out, he'd want to keep them sweet and compliant in the roles he'd assigned them! And would he have defended her to his mistress, saying she was a brilliant wife?

Another silly question!

Cat took a wobbly step away from him but the pressure of his hands simply increased, bringing her closer to the hard arch of his pelvis. His body heat scorched her. Her heart thumped madly and she gasped as she tried to pull enough air into her starved lungs to enable her to tell him to stop this hateful pretence, but all that emerged from her parched lips was a tiny, despairing groan.

'Don't be sad, *cara*,' he said, obviously mistaking that distressed little sound for something else entirely. His voice was soft now, silken and husky at the same time, and his eyes were drenched with concern. It might be spurious but from where she was standing it looked bone-weakeningly real, she thought distractedly. 'I do know how you feel. I, too, grieve for our lost child.' He drew her gently within the circle of his arms, one hand easing her head into the accommodating breadth of his shoulder, the other stroking her rigid spine until against all common sense she felt her whole body relaxing into him.

Her eyes filled with hot tears and, almost hesitantly, her arms curved around him, the palms of her hands flat against his shoulder blades. However much she hated and despised him for the emotional turmoil he had put her through she loved the feel of him, the strength of bone, the perfectly honed muscles, the warm satin of his skin. He was addictive, like a drug, and she was hooked, she acknowledged shakily, despising herself far more than she had thought she despised him.

And as he murmured soft words of comfort in Italian, surely the most seductive language in the world, his clean, warm breath feathered against the long line of her neck and made her tremble.

He sounded so sincere she could almost believe he cared. Fool that she was, she wanted to believe, she needed to. She shifted slightly closer, she really couldn't help herself, feeling the inevitable pool of liquid heat between her thighs, feeling the answering, hardening response of him against the shimmering, needy fire that was building up inside her body.

She had never doubted that he'd been devastated when she'd lost their baby, that he genuinely mourned the tiny lost life. But now her mind was frantically grasping at straws, holding on to the belief that perhaps he really cared for her, too.

'There will be other babies for us,' he murmured deeply, and Cat shivered as she forced herself to take that in, her mind recoiling and then finally understanding.

How could she have forgotten the way things really were, clung on to the illusion of his concern and caring? She felt humiliated and deeply ashamed of herself. She pulled away from him, her movements stiff and clumsy, her eyes haunted in her pale face.

He meant to do his damnedest to get her pregnant

again and she, like a dutiful little wife, was meant to go along with it. That was what all this sickening pretence at closeness and caring had been about! Where had he been when she'd needed him most— touring the length and breadth of Italy, staying in glamorous top hotels and having a wonderful time— with his mistress!

'Leave me alone. Just go!'

Her face felt so tight she had to force the words out through her teeth. And she flinched as if he'd hit her when he gazed down at her with those bitter-chocolate eyes and soothed, 'You don't mean that. You are still understandably upset. Raffacani warned me your hormones could still be all over the place. But I am here now to help you overcome this.'

Oh, was he? Was he really? And none of this was his fault—of course not! Heaven forfend! It was all down to her and her hormones!

Cat snatched in a ragged breath and then exploded, 'I meant it—I want you to leave me alone! I had Maria make a bed up for you in the master suite. You'll find your things in there, too.'

She'd discovered them after lunch while Aldo and Iolanda had been closeted in the library, supposedly going over the facts and figures the wretched woman had keyed in on her laptop. Cat's need to clear both him and his clothes out of her space had been violent and immediate.

Her wishes hadn't been consulted; he'd simply taken it for granted that he would share her bed. Like any normal husband. But he wasn't a normal husband, was he?

And the way a wash of hot, dull colour spread over his hard, high cheekbones, his stiffly polite, 'As you wish,' as he swung on his heel and strode out, cut no ice with her. She watched his exit through narrowed, glittering eyes then wondered why her throat seized up and a torrent of tears ran down her cheeks.

How she could be expected to sleep when her mind kept running round in circles, Cat didn't know. Grumpily, when a squinting look at the tiny gilded bedside clock told her it was past three o'clock, she gave up the attempt and slid out of bed, padding over to one of the tall windows to gaze out at the purity of the moonlit landscape, trying to calm her mind.

But it would keep churning, homing in on memories; presenting each in vivid Technicolor before skittering on to the next.

Their fairy-tale wedding in Florence. A besotted bride in a beautiful cream silk dress. Aldo tall and impossibly handsome in his morning suit, looking for all the world as if he was truly in love with the woman he had decided to make his wife. And Gramps, pleased as punch, acquainting himself with his nephew Astorre and his grand Roman wife—Aldo's parents—happy to be welcomed back into the bosom of his Italian family.

Cat pressed her fingertips to her throbbing temples. She wished Gramps were still here, so that she could turn to him for advice and comfort. Wished he hadn't insisted—despite all offers to the contrary—on returning to England, Bonnie and the memories of his Alice and Anna, her mother, the daughter they had so tragically lost all those long years ago.

Cat wanted her mother. And her father. She had been too young when they'd died to remember either of them. But she wanted them now. She, who had always been so independent, wanted someone to lean on. Loving Aldo had turned her into a wreck. And she hated the feeling!

And still the unwanted memories came, mind pictures she couldn't dispel, no matter how hard she tried to shut them out...

The honeymoon in the house above Portofino, the vine-covered mountains as a backdrop, the fabulous view over the spectacular coastline. The long, shatteringly intimate nights, the sun-drenched days, wandering hand in hand down to the yacht-filled harbour, past the pretty, pastel-coloured houses set in gardens filled with a riot of blossoms, eating locally prepared delicacies, toasting each other with crisp Ligurian wine...

And the way it had begun. Begun as soon as she'd set eyes on him. The sexual chemistry had been mindboggling. But she could have handled that, written it off as the entirely natural reaction of a young, healthy, celibate female to a superb specimen of manhood. A specimen whose eyes had promised paradise.

But she hadn't been able to write off what had

happened in her studio apartment. From the moment he'd taken her in his arms and kissed her she'd been lost. She had kissed him back, it had been hot and torrid, hands everywhere, breathing fast and fevered, and she'd been lost in abandonment, his for the taking, and he had tasted of heaven, of desire, and she had sunk into him, offering all that she was, all that she had, and afterwards, towards dawn at the end of that long, shatteringly ecstatic night, she had known with every fibre of her love-drenched, expertly ravished body that she could teach him to love her. Given time and patience.

It had been her secret weapon. Secret because he had said he wouldn't marry a woman who claimed to be madly in love with him because emotional demands such as that would complicate his life.

So she had never let him know that she adored the very ground he walked on. She had matched his greedy passion of the night and never even hinted at the dagger of hurt deep within her heart when he acted like a polite, considerate stranger away from the earth-shattering magic of the bedroom.

Telling herself she was in for the long haul—such a self-controlled, self-confident individual wouldn't be quick to admit he'd been wrong, admit he could fall in love—she had held her tongue, hidden her feelings and set about turning herself into the type of wife she guessed he wanted. Cool, in control, chic and sophisticated. Almost the complete opposite of who and what she really was.

And she could have handled it. If it hadn't been for the drip of poison.

Iolanda's poison.

Cat ground her teeth together. Her whole body was in pain. She paced the floor, her movements savage, until she snapped to a halt in mid-turn.

What if it wasn't true? What if none of it was true?

Was Iolanda spiteful enough to make up such terrible lies?

You bet she was!

To begin with, Cat had refused to believe a word of what the poisonous woman had said. But events had forced her to change her opinion. What if those telling events—his moving to another bedroom as soon as her pregnancy had been confirmed, his increasing absences from their home, his complete absence after her miscarriage—had been mere coincidences?

He hadn't wanted to make love to her and put their child at risk, or so he'd said. A very unenlightened belief, but one he could genuinely have held perhaps? And his prolonged business trek with his executive assistant—well, that could have been genuine too.

He had business interests all over Italy, huge responsibilities. He had once told her that he insisted on taking complete control over every area and delegated very little, confessing wryly that he had become something of a workaholic.

And he hadn't neglected her entirely during the past eight weeks, had he? He'd phoned her twice, sometimes three times a week, and sent postcards from each area he'd visited—usually with some humorous comment. And once, by special messenger, a pair of fabulous emerald earrings with the scrawled comment, 'You don't have to make your own now! Enjoy!'

She was weakening. And muddled. And the only way to clear up the mess was to ask him outright, demand the absolute truth.

Was Iolanda his mistress?

If he categorically denied it and fired his executive assistant for telling lies and making mischief then she would do her utmost to make a go of their marriage, even though it didn't seem likely that he'd change his entrenched opinion that falling in love was for idiots, because at least she would know that he had enough respect for her to stay faithful.

She should have asked him earlier, when he'd followed her to her bedroom, she acknowledged as she slipped into her wrap and tied the belt around her narrow waist. But pride had stopped her, not to mention despair and the out-and-out hurting of her battered heart.

It was the early hours of the morning and he'd be sound asleep but she was going to have to wake him. Now that the need to know had finally and with much effort burst through her tight-lipped, brooding suffering she couldn't wait another second.

The suite of rooms she had banished him to was about as far as it was possible to be from her tower rooms and she took the long, thickly carpeted corridor that branched from the main staircase and was pretty sure the mad beating of her heart would suffocate her long before she reached her destination.

Wall sconces, placed at intervals between the closed doors along the silent corridors that now seemed never-ending, threw muted pools of welcome light and as she reached the last corner, the final stretch, the door to Aldo's suite opened quietly and Iolanda, clad in something revealingly diaphanous and skimpy, slipped out, her lovely face flushed.

Cat's bare feet came to an abrupt full stop, everything inside her curling up in a painful, icy knot with the horror of what she was seeing. And after a momentary hesitation when the other woman looked as if she had been turned into stone, Iolanda's mouth curved in a cat's-got-the-cream smile as she clutched the tiny packet she was holding between her pert little breasts.

No need to ask what she was doing, or what that packet contained, Cat thought jaggedly as her stomach lurched over nauseously and her knees turned to water, wobbling alarmingly as Iolanda, putting on that definitely superior smile again, advised, 'I wouldn't bother if I were you. You can take my word for it, Aldo definitely won't be able to accommodate you right now.'

And swept past her, heading for her own room, trailing wafts of heavy perfume, her low, husky laugh more than Cat could possibly bear.

She was shaking, sick with shock as she forced her rubbery legs to carry her very slowly back to her own rooms, making it to the bathroom just in time before she was violently and wretchedly sick.

At least her question was now answered, she told herself as she rinsed her mouth out with cold water. She'd had all the confirmation she needed without having to ask her rotten husband if he was being unfaithful, and inadvertently revealing how deeply and permanently she'd fallen in love with him on that fatal night when he'd made love to her for the first time.

She'd been spared that ultimate indignity, which was the only thing that could be said for the horror of what she'd witnessed.

Slowly, she made it back into the bedroom and coldly smoothed out the bundle of hot chaos that was her brain.

She would make him pay for breaking her heart. She would make him pay in spades!

CHAPTER FOUR

'THAT colour always suited you. I like it,' Aldo approved warmly as Cat finally presented herself at the breakfast table in front of the open French windows later that morning.

The last morning she would be sharing anything with him, she reminded herself hollowly as she poured coffee from the pot and took it with her to the edge of the terrace that overlooked the tumbling, flower-packed gardens.

Devious, lying, rotten creep! She reinforced her rock-bottom opinion of the wretched man who called himself her husband. How dared he pay empty compliments when he'd spent the best part of last night having wild sex with his mistress?

She didn't trust herself to speak to him, let alone sit at the table with him. At least Iolanda didn't seem to have surfaced yet. Catching up on the beauty sleep she'd missed last night, was she?

And as soon as she'd had her much-needed shot of caffeine she'd tell him what she'd decided.

And of course he didn't like the in-your-face vivid scarlet of her short cotton skirt and matching sleeveless cropped top; that was partly why she'd chosen it.

It wasn't chic, understated or even remotely sophisticated! And the long, searingly yellow chiffon scarf she'd tied tightly around her waist to keep the now too-large skirt from dropping round her ankles would be viewed as an affront to his impeccable good taste. Even now he was probably squinting, reaching for his shades.

Which was precisely why she'd delved into the depths of the huge hanging cupboard to find what she could of her pre-transformation clothes and had been already dressed in the most flamboyant things she could find when Rosa arrived with the tray of morning tea.

Ignoring the other woman's tut of disapproval, Cat had dismissed her. Never again would she allow her hair to be sculptured and tortured into sleek submission or dress in the sort of classic gear designed for the seriously sophisticated. From now on Aldo could look to Iolanda for his idea of female perfection. She was reverting to type! She was her own woman again, not his!

'Aren't you eating?' The soft, dark-honey voice that came from directly behind her now was threaded through with what Cat supposed was meant to convey husbandly concern and she guessed that it wasn't entirely manufactured. He'd want her fit and healthy when he got her pregnant—that was the main consideration and she'd do well to remember it.

Apart from that he had little interest in her.

As witness what had happened last night, she thought on a renewed spurt of crushing anger. His

wife had as good as booted him out of her bedroom
so he'd merely shrugged those impressive shoulders
and arranged for his mistress to share his banishment.
No skin off his arrogant nose!

'Where is she?' Cat ignored his question and replaced her cup on its saucer. It rattled alarmingly. She
put it smartly down on the stone balustrading, out of
harm's way.

Aldo, moving closer, asked with ominous smoothness, 'Who is ''she''?'

Cat took a long, hopefully calming breath. The air
was hot and arid and scented with the wild thyme and
fennel that grew on the stony hillside. 'The Cardinale
woman,' she managed frigidly. No way, no way
would she let him know how very much he'd hurt
her. If he knew how deeply she'd loved him it would
be the final ignominy. She'd suffered enough, hadn't
she?

Aldo stepped into her line of vision. Cat shivered
despite the hot August sun on her bare arms. Dressed
in light fawn chinos and a casual coffee-coloured
lawn shirt, he looked monumentally devastating, his
dark eyes veiled by the thick, curving sweep of lashes
that failed to completely hide the hard golden glitter
of biting impatience.

She tipped her head, presenting him with her profile as he voiced his displeasure. 'Iolanda left an hour
ago. I arranged for Sergio to drive her back to
Florence.' His tone became glacial. 'Iolanda is a
highly valued business colleague as well as a friend.

I expect you to remember that and show some respect.'

Unable to respond to that without blowing her top explosively, Cat ignored his more conciliatory invitation, 'Why don't we start the morning again and have breakfast together?' swung round on her heels and sailed back through the French windows, resolutely bypassing the white linen-covered table set with rolls and honey and a huge bowl of fresh fruit.

'I'm leaving you,' she said clearly so there could be no mistake. 'I want a divorce.'

A tiny pulse of utter silence, then, 'What did you say?' he delivered in a tone of utter dryness and Cat paused in her dignified retreat, and that was a huge mistake, she recognised sickly as his overwhelmingly masculine and coldly furious body suddenly appeared in front of her, blocking her path.

'You are not going deaf, as far as I know,' she cast at him brittly, her chin up, her eyes narrowed with emerald disdain as she fiercely reminded herself that she could handle the two-timing brute. 'You heard me. I want a divorce.'

'Why?' His mouth was set in a hard, enraged line, but a genuine query drew a line between his eyes. Was he shocked to discover, probably for the very first time in his life, that what he wanted was not always what he got?

'Because I don't like our marriage,' she answered flatly.

She was desperately hanging on to her by now precarious cool. Start to tell him that she knew of his affair with Iolanda, display her hurt and jealousy, and she would end up raving, going to pieces right in front of him. Her closely guarded secret would be out, laid raw and bleeding in front of him.

The realisation that she loved him, had since she'd first laid eyes on him, would make her look a fool and give him the ammunition he needed to sweet-talk her into staying with him. Making promises he had no intention of keeping to get what he wanted: financial assets to add to masses he already had, a dutiful and gullible wife, children. That was never going to happen; she wouldn't let it. She would make sure her secret was safe.

Disconcertingly, he stood aside to let her pass unhindered. And tears stung her eyes as she took the stairs to her tower rooms. Was he prepared to let her go so easily? Had their marriage meant so little to him? Had she?

Obviously.

Well, she already knew that, didn't she? Senseless to get in a state about it. She hadn't really wanted him to try to talk her out of her decision—surely she hadn't! Besides, she'd be free of him before too long, she reminded herself. Back in England, able to get on with the rest of her life.

Gramps would be furious with her, that went without saying, but surely when he knew the full story he would be firmly on her side, she consoled herself as she dug the clothes she'd brought to Italy with her from where Rosa had consigned them to the far depths of the wardrobe. She wanted no reminders of her life here; she'd leave all the expensive designer gear behind.

Just as she'd leave her heart behind? a nasty little voice enquired inside her head. She blotted it out vehemently. She hated Aldo now. Falling in love with him had been a highly costly mistake in emotional terms. And as long as she lived she would never repeat it.

Aldo's attitude was the right one. Falling in love was for fools.

Her passport was somewhere. She couldn't get back to England without it. Maybe she'd put it in one of the dressing-table drawers, or Rosa had. She really couldn't remember. She'd been in a state of shock and utter misery when she and the luggage Aldo had personally insisted on packing for her had arrived here shortly after her miscarriage, not really aware of, or caring about, what was going on around her.

'Looking for something?'

The shock of hearing his voice froze her fingers as they scrabbled through the contents of her underwear drawer. Cat felt her colour come and go and her spine prickled with tension. Somehow she had to control herself, stay cool. She had to!

Turning slowly, she said very precisely, 'My passport.' She pushed a wayward strand of copper-coloured hair away from her forehead with the back of her hand, praying she looked calm and collected even though she was churning with anger, jealousy and the sense of bitter betrayal. 'When Sergio returns I want him to drive me to Pisa Airport,' she stated with a coolness that quietly amazed her.

And was even more amazed when he answered her demand by pacing right up to her, his smile gentle but with a definite touch of the predator about it.

What he found to smile about in this ghastly situation she couldn't imagine but soon found out when he said with cool warning, 'No one will drive you anywhere and your passport is in the safe in Florence, along with mine and our wedding certificate. You are my wife, and what is mine I keep. Always remember that, Caterina.'

He was still smiling, that was the worst part. Even worse than the problem of getting herself back to Florence to pick up her passport. She wished he wasn't standing so close to her, close enough for her to inhale his cool, lemony aftershave, to feel his body heat. It was physically unsettling.

But she wouldn't retreat, not by a single inch. He mustn't know how threatened she felt by his nearness, how he made her whole body tingle, every cell going on red alert, every nerve-end screaming a warning.

Cat stood her ground so firmly she was proud of herself, her words sounding harsh as she pushed them through her teeth. 'You can't keep me where I don't want to be. Short of chaining me to the bedpost.'

'Now, there's an idea!' he came back softly, his smile widening to a grin. A grin which slid into

wicked sultriness as his bitter-chocolate eyes imprisoned her gaze with blatant sensuality. He had hyp-
notic eyes, she thought with a deep shudder. She
couldn't look away, even though her tired brain told
her she must. She felt as if she were drowning. She
felt her lips part as she struggled to pull air into her
starving lungs.

'But I don't need to use chains, do I?' A hand came
up to touch the dimple at the side of her mouth, lingering for one tummy-clenching moment before dropping away. 'There are much more pleasant ways of
keeping you with me. Yes?' A lean hand reached for
the trailing ends of the long yellow scarf. And tugged.

Cat's body was on fire. Now a mere whisper away
from the lean masculinity of his, she didn't know
what to do with herself, couldn't have stepped away
even if she could summon the will-power to want to.
He had her trapped, as much by her own deeply regrettable lack of defences against him as by his far
superior strength. And when he'd spoken there had
been a strand of powerful satisfaction in his voice, so
something about her must have betrayed her.

She made a tiny sound of humiliation at the back
of her throat and Aldo dipped his darkly handsome
head closer and warned softly, 'But to cover all con-
tingencies, even if you do manage to hike the five
miles down to the village you will get no further. One
phone call from me will make sure that no one, but
no one, will be willing to drive you anywhere.'

Another tug on the yellow scarf around her waist

brought them into direct contact. The thrust of his pelvis, the hard wall of his chest pressing against her breasts, his thighs against her thighs. Her mouth went dry and the old familiar throbbing started up deep inside her.

Desperately, Cat tried to mentally gather the knowledge that he was a despicable, unfaithful, un-caring rat but her brain was spinning so dizzily she couldn't hold a single Aldo-damning thought in her head for longer than a nanosecond.

'You are mine and you stay mine.' He dropped the scarf and clamped his hands on either side of her narrow waist in one smooth, authoritative movement, pulling her weakly unresistant body hard against his, his gorgeous mouth so close to hers that his warm, clean breath feathered over her lips, making them tremble and feel almost unbearably sensitive. 'And you go nowhere until I know what you meant when you said you didn't like our marriage. But for now there are things I know you do like, *cara*.'

His hands slid up her ribcage and curved over her aching breasts as he slowly explored the outline of her engorged nipples. Sultry heat spread through her entire body, converging hectically on what his clever hands were doing to her. 'You can explain what displeases you later and I will remedy it,' he promised with husky-voiced male arrogance, his eyes dropping to watch the movement of his fingers as he began the task of slipping the buttons down the front of her top from their moorings.

He was going to make love to her, Cat knew that. She could stop it by flinging his infidelity in his face. Or she could let it happen, take what her feeble body was yearning for. It was her choice.

Or no choice at all. She gave a harsh inhalation of breath as he parted the fabric, exposing the hedonistic invitation of her peaking breasts. An invitation he took with an avidity that swept her to dizzy heights of ecstasy and pushed her mental flailings for autonomy right out of existence.

This need for him was elemental, raw and passionate. It had been her undoing from the first moment she'd set eyes on him. That was her last coherent thought as he gave each breast individual and tormenting attention. And then, as so many times in the past, she was actively helping him, her fingers undoing his shirt buttons, her concentration feverish and intense.

As she exposed his perfectly honed naked torso to her drugged eyes and ran her fingers over the sleek, bronzed skin Cat moaned softly and he bent forward, taking her breath into his mouth as he enforced with soft determination, 'You are mine,' before plundering her lips with a hot, hungry urgency that had her reeling, responding with her own feverish demands, her hips echoing the blindingly erotic movement of his, her fingernails digging into the taut, heated skin of his firmly muscled back as he walked her backwards to the huge bed.

The last of their clothing was jettisoned in a flurry

of impatient hands, the bed covers flung to the floor as their bodies writhed, mouths clinging together, and their lovemaking was savage, almost, Cat thought with a wild, exultant cry, as if they needed to punish each other.

But later, and after, it was gentle, dreamy, slow and thoughtful, and as Cat drifted into an exhausted sleep she wondered if she would experience anything so out of this world and perfect ever again.

It was very far from perfect, was Cat's immediate thought when she woke abruptly. Letting Aldo seduce her senseless all over again had been nothing but a self-destructive mistake.

From the angle of the sun as it flooded the room with soft light she could tell it was late afternoon. They had been in bed together all day—she could just imagine the staff's knowing smiles when neither of them had been seen, not even for lunch. Her face went red with embarrassment and shame for the weakness of her will.

She had planned on being out of here by this time on the first leg of her journey back to England.

Only Aldo had insisted she wasn't going anywhere. He'd move heaven and earth to stop her.

Cat shifted gingerly. The last thing she wanted to do was wake him. For the first time ever he'd held her close to him after they were both too sated to do anything other than fall into a deep and drugging sleep. Normally he turned his back on her, shutting her out.

Ironic, really, she decided grimly as she carefully extricated herself from the imprisonment of his arms. Once she would have rejoiced, taken the way he held her as an indication that he wanted a close, intimate contact beyond the act of sex itself.

Now she saw it for what it was. Imprisonment. Exactly that.

'You are mine. What is mine I keep.' His earlier words echoed sharply in her head.

But why? He certainly didn't love her. She was a mere convenience, one that could easily be replaced. He couldn't even feel affection for her, let alone respect. Carrying on with his mistress was evidence of that!

As she moved out of the room her bare feet hit the cool white marble of the *en suite* floor and she paused, pressing her fingertips against her burning forehead. Why would he be so adamant about holding on to an unloved wife who had categorically stated that she wanted a divorce?

She would have staked her life on him letting her go with about as much regret as he'd wipe a smear of mud from the sole of one of his hand-crafted shoes. His pride and arrogance would have demanded nothing less.

Under normal circumstances she would have opted for a long soak in a warm, scented bath to soothe away the little aches and stiffnesses occasioned by long hours of intense lovemaking, but this afternoon she really needed to get a move-on, clear her head and plan her way out of the stranglehold Aldo had on her.

Never mind Aldo's feudal power over the local villagers, it wasn't beyond her ingenuity to look further afield, find a taxi firm which would be willing to send a driver out here—preferably with someone riding shotgun!

The stinging needles of the icy-cold shower took her breath away but it helped the penny to finally drop and gave her the stark answer to the questions she'd asked herself earlier.

Of course! It was obvious when she looked at it from his viewpoint. A divorce would mean she could claim a large chunk of his assets and, as far as he knew, the loss of those shares and the inheritance that would eventually come to her.

What was his he kept; he'd never said a truer word! She mentally derided her slow mental processes as she dried herself briskly to get her circulation moving again after nearly freezing under that prolonged douche of icy water. She should have cottoned on immediately.

Aldo Patrucco, head of a huge and highly successful business empire, had married for purely mercenary reasons, as many of his ancestors before him had done. Fact.

His avarice meant he would do anything to keep her and the assets she came with—even to the extent of expending all that energy making love to her, proving that he could turn her on with just one look. Fact.

Well, she didn't aim to be the captive of his avarice, she told herself staunchly as she blow-dried her hair until it stood away from her face like a wild and crinkly halo. And she could have saved herself a whole heap of heartbreak and anguish if she'd turned down his marriage proposal and told him not to worry. Her inheritance would go to him, lock, stock, barrel and wretched shares. Gramps had been very firm about what he intended to do if she'd refused to go along with his mad idea.

She would bet her last bent farthing that had he had that information Aldo would have made good and sure she didn't accept him, most definitely would not have turned on all that considerable sex appeal and seduced her into saying yes. He would have taken her refusal and turned thankfully on his heels, safe in the knowledge that he would eventually get back those shares without going to the bother of marrying anyone!

He could have carried on his nasty affair—with the vile Iolanda and who knew how many others?—without the fear of being found out by a jealous wife!

Aware that her blood pressure was threatening to blow the top of her head off, Cat told herself to cool it. There was a way out of this mess; of course there was.

All she had to do was be very adult about it. Tell her two-timing husband that if he agreed to a divorce, to let her go, she would ask for nothing from him. She needed only assure him that she would sign any document agreeing to that to have him moving heaven and earth to get her on the first available flight back to England. After she'd signed on the dotted line, of course!

Remember, too, to assure him that Gramps would see the break-up of their marriage as being all her fault. He'd certainly been more interested in closing the family circle after the rift of his own creating than he had been in her future welfare or happiness, so he'd view the divorce as just as reprehensible, if not worse, than an initial refusal to marry the man of his choice and disinherit her in favour of Aldo as he had threatened.

That still had the power to hurt. Badly. Her eyes glinted with tears and there was a lump the size of a house in her throat as she crept quietly back into the bedroom. She swallowed noisily and then, panic-stricken, held her breath.

But thankfully Aldo seemed to be still asleep. Sprawled out on his back, stark naked. Cat dragged her eyes away. He was stunning. Her throat closed up as the lingering intimate ache at the juncture of her thighs suddenly and sharply intensified.

She could throttle him for having this power over her and she had to get dressed as quickly and quietly as possible. Naked, she felt spectacularly vulnerable. As she acknowledged with a huge feeling of shame, he only had to look at her, say one word, to have her weakly giving in to the desire he had brought to scorching life.

One look at her nakedness with those dark, sexy eyes, one velvet word—

'*Cara*, what are you doing?'

Cat froze, her heart tumbling about inside her chest. That slow, honeyed tone made every sensitised inch of her skin burn and prickle with unwanted, shameful excitement. She hated herself for what her louse of a husband could do to her!

And he could see what she was doing, she thought dementedly. Hopping about on one foot trying to get her knickers on!

Arms flailing wildly, she lost her balance and one of Aldo's hands snaked out to steady her, to drag her onto the rumpled bed with him, her white satin briefs round her ankles.

'You don't need these.' He disentangled the scrap of fabric and dropped it to the carpet, his big naked body partly covering hers as she lay spreadeagled against the pillows. His gorgeous face was a mere inch or two away from her own; she could see the tiny golden lights deep in his dark-as-sin eyes and stopped breathing.

One strong hand held both of hers above her head and one hair-roughened thigh imprisoned her slender lower limbs. 'I intend, my little darling—' a lightly provocative brush of his mouth against her parted lips '—to keep you in bed—' another kiss, as light as a butterfly's wings, on the tip of her neat nose '—na-

ked. Until—' his long, sensual mouth found the point
of her jaw just below the lobe of her ear '—you tell
me—' and trailed a line of shimmering fire down the
taut line of her throat '—why you had a tantrum and
said you didn't like our marriage.'

Tantrum! How dared he speak to her as if she were
a simpering child? Her treacherous body, which had
been on the point of melting completely and shame-
fully beneath the seductive onslaught of his mouth,
bristled, a bundle of furious energy prepared to fight
him off every inch of the way.

Aldo shifted, presumably sensing a battle he had
no intention of losing, Cat thought agitatedly, everything inside her going haywire as she felt his erection
against the quivering flesh of her tummy. Heat pooled
through the centre of her femininity, began to pulse,
and, desperation fuelling her, she tried to clamp her
thighs together but the domineering strength of his
thigh prevented any defensive movement at all.

And then she found she didn't want to move at all
as his tantalising mouth moved lower, finding the val-
ley between her breasts, his voice a wicked seduction
in itself as he covered her unbearably sensitised skin
with kisses and murmured throatily, 'For me, our
marriage is good. You are so beautiful, *cara*. And for
you, you have me, you live in luxury, you will never
want for anything. What is there not to like about
that? You have everything I promised you when we
agreed to marry. And the sex is the greatest. Yes?'

As if to prove his point he slid a hand down to the

soft copper curls at the apex of her sex and, as if satisfied by her wriggle of immediate and unconquerable response, he whispered, 'We have shared a sadness in the loss of our baby but I am with you now, as I planned it, and I promise to make everything perfect.'

Make another baby! That was what the unfaithful wretch meant!

That finally got through to her, galvanised her treacherously weak body into raging action. He would have sex with her until he was sure she was pregnant again—and then take off! That was his vile plan!

Languid, nerveless hands became tight fists, fists to punch holes in those wide, dominating shoulders; the body that had been supine, aching for his, squirmed like an eel, taking him by surprise as she slithered off the bed, snatching up a long-discarded sheet and wrapping it tightly around her tense body.

There would be nothing adult or calm about what she threw at this…this monster now! Of course he was content with this marriage—a dutiful wife, kept in pampered luxury, responsive to his dutiful attentions, expected to turn a blind eye to his sordid, ongoing affair!

And pushing his immense wealth, the luxuries she was supposed to be grateful for, under her nose was the very last straw. If he'd loved her then she would have been happy to dress in rags, share a cardboard box with him and wash in a bucket!

'I have something to say to you,' she hissed at him,

all fired up to let him have both barrels—his infidelity, the divorce, everything—hardly hearing her own words through the violent roar of her own thoughts that was drowning out everything else.

She could see, though, see the frowning intensity of his eyes as they stabbed into her own. See the way he had swung upright and was sitting on the edge of the bed, his face shadowed and grim as if he couldn't understand what was going on here.

See the way he reached out one hand to her, his mouth parting as though he was about to say something then clamping shut again, his frown deepening alarmingly as he looked towards the door.

He bit out, 'Yes?' his voice blistering, and Cat turned. If Rosa had knocked before entering she hadn't heard her through the angry roar of blood in her brain.

'I'm sorry, *signor*.' Rosa went red, obviously embarrassed by her employer's naked state. She was holding one of the cordless phones. She held it out to Cat. 'A message for the *signora*; I think it's important. Otherwise I wouldn't have dreamed of—'

'Forget it.' Aldo's injunction was tersely impatient. He rose to his feet, magnificently male, magnificently unembarrassed as he strode through to the bathroom, leaving Rosa to scuttle away and Cat to give her attention to the slim, silver-coloured instrument in her hand.

It was Bonnie. Her grandfather's housekeeper sounded at the end of her tether.

'You must come—he'd want you to. They've just taken him to hospital and—'

'Who?' Cat suddenly went icily cold, the blistering heat of her anger towards her errant husband washed away with a swamping wave of fear. She already knew the answer.

'Your grandfather. The ambulance. I phoned them. It's a heart attack. There were these paramedics. They said he would be fine but it looked very bad to me. He was asking for you. He wanted to tell you something; I knew it was bothering him and—'

'Bonnie,' Cat's voice was firm even though her whole body was trembling with reaction, 'I'll be with you just as soon as I can. Hire a taxi—anything—just go and see him and tell him that. And Bonnie...' her voice cracked '...tell him I love him.'

CHAPTER FIVE

AS THE Patrucco company jet began its descent to Birmingham International Aldo took Cat's clenched hands and gently straightened out her white-knuckled fingers.

'Try to relax. A hired car is waiting. If the traffic is kind you will be with your grandfather in a little over an hour. Maybe an hour and a half.'

Cat gave him a wan smile and made no attempt to pull her hands away from the comforting strength of his. She knew she shouldn't need her unfaithful, self-seeking husband, not in any capacity, but to be brutally honest with herself she did. She didn't know what she would have done without him today—run around like a headless chicken, she supposed glumly.

Aldo had taken over the phone, making three or four terse, authoritative calls, packed for them both and almost before she'd had time to draw breath he was driving them to Pisa

Someone from his company had been waiting at the airport with the passports he'd obviously been instructed to collect from the house in Florence. Every single thing had gone like well-oiled clockwork. She hadn't had to do a thing except get herself dressed and notify the staff of their imminent departure.

She would always be deeply grateful for the way he'd calmly taken charge, organised everything with no fuss whatsoever and not a second's waste of precious time, endlessly grateful for his quiet reassurances, his immediate understanding of how frightened and nerve-rackingly anxious she was feeling.

If only things were different, she thought wretchedly as the transfer from the jet to the waiting car was accomplished with a smooth lack of delay. If only he'd given Iolanda her marching orders before they'd married and stayed faithful to her she would have loved this man until her dying breath, lived for him, for his pleasure, even though she knew he would never really love her. She would have settled for affection, fidelity and respect. As it was she had none of these things.

Tears were glittering on the tips of her long, sweeping lashes as he settled in the driving seat beside her and leaned over to check her seat belt.

'Don't,' he pleaded thickly as he brushed the drops away with the tips of his fingers. 'I can't bear to see you cry. We have no way of knowing how severe Domenico's attack was until we speak to his consultant. Until then we must be optimistic. He is in good hands, remember, and these days, *cara*, miracles can be worked.'

Cat nodded mutely as, with a final intent appraisal of her drawn features, he fastened his own seat belt and turned the key in the ignition. Her tears, that time, had been for the ending of their marriage, but he wasn't to know that. By unspoken agreement they had put everything on hold, not mentioned her demand for a divorce since the news about Gramps's heart attack had come through.

Late at night the motorway was relatively quiet and the powerful saloon simply ate up the miles, and Aldo invited, 'Tell me about your grandfather's housekeeper—Bonnie, isn't it?'

'Ellen Boniface,' Cat supplied, leaning back against the leather headrest and closing her eyes. 'Why? What about her?'

'Is she a fixture?'

'As fixed as they come.'

He couldn't really want to be regaled with information about Bonnie but probably thought that getting her to talk about the elderly housekeeper would shift her mind away from her worries about Gramps. In many ways Aldo was a fine man, but in the most important way, as far as she was concerned, he was deeply flawed.

But she didn't want to think about that, either, so she pushed it to the back of her mind to be brought out later when she'd truly satisfied herself that Gramps was going to be OK.

'No family of her own?'

For her sake he was still trying to draw her out on a subject he could have no real interest in, so she'd do him the courtesy of going along with it, even though it was an effort to talk at all.

'Apparently not. Bonnie never married and, initially, my grandparents hired her to help look after me after my parents were killed. I was only a baby. When I got less of a handful—'

'I can't imagine you ever being anything other than a handful!' he commented with dry amusement. 'I can imagine you as a complete tomboy and spoiled rotten.'

'I saw a fair bit of action,' she concurred readily, remembering the scrapes she'd got into while she'd been growing up and the whole of the countryside had been her playground, casting a glancing look at the darkened austerity of his profile as she told him tremulously, 'I don't know about being spoiled rotten, but I do know I was loved.'

Her throat closed up; she couldn't say any more. She'd been surrounded by love in her childhood but Gran was gone now and Gramps had demonstrated that healing the rift with his Italian relatives counted for more with him than she did and that had left a wound that would take a long time to heal over.

And Aldo had never loved her at all.

But she couldn't blame him for that, she counselled herself with painful honesty. He had never once tried to fool her; he'd told her quite openly that he didn't believe in the condition. The fault was all hers for naïvely believing she could change his mind and make him fall in love with her.

The warm pressure of his hand as it briefly and comfortingly closed over hers startled her then filled her with a deep and yearning ache. He was being too kind; she couldn't bear it! And she had to swallow hard and pull in a harsh breath to enable her to answer at all when he continued to question lightly, 'I guess your Bonnie grew into your family?'

'Absolutely.' Her voice sounded choked, but she soldiered on. 'My grandparents relied on her and she on them. After Gran died Bonnie and Gramps got even more dependent on each other.' She frowned and chewed on the corner of her lip. 'I haven't given her a single thought for hours—she'll be rattling around in that big house on her own, worried out of her wits.'

'Then contact her now. I should have thought about it sooner,' he admitted tersely. 'She'll be glad to hear we're well on our way.' He produced a slim mobile phone from the inside pocket of the fawn linen jacket he was wearing. 'And tell her to get some sleep. We're booked into an hotel near the hospital so she won't have to wait up for us, or worry about feeding us.' And at Cat's sharp intake of breath he added, 'I thought it best for you to be a few hundred yards away rather than fifteen or so miles.'

Cat's throat was achingly tight as she dialled. She wished he wouldn't be so damned thoughtful and considerate! It only made her love him more and she really couldn't afford to!

Bonnie answered on the first ring. Her voice tearful, she explained that she hadn't been allowed to visit, but she had asked the person she'd spoken to to pass on Cat's earlier messages, and when the call ended after five minutes of gentle reassurances from Cat, who was feeling far from reassured herself, the elderly housekeeper sounded more relaxed.

'Not long now,' Aldo commented as the call ended, his voice gruff. 'Thankfully, the hospital's signed on every intersection.'

Cat nodded mutely, her hands twisting together in her lap. He'd been brilliant—since leaving the motorway he'd only once asked her to consult the road map. It was just a pity that he couldn't be as good at being a husband as he was at everything else!

But that anguished thought, together with everything else, flew right out of her head as they entered the hospital environs. Her stomach clenched in a sickening knot of dread.

And only Aldo's strong arm around her waist kept her upright as they made their way to the Intensive Care Unit and only will-power kept her from bursting into tears when the door was unlocked and she was admitted alone with strict instructions not to make a fuss, or a noise, and only stay for two minutes.

Gramps looked so frail and shrunken, his face a distressing shade of grey. He was hooked to a monitor, a drip, and was being fed oxygen, and the humming of machines in the otherwise utter silence seemed unearthly.

She snagged in a breath. He was sleeping. Wanting to transfer some of her strength to him, she touched his hand and willed him to get better. And as his eyelids fluttered open she leant forward and kissed his forehead and whispered, 'Love you, Gramps. Rest now and I'll see you in the morning.' And saw him smile before closing his eyes again and slipping back into sleep.

Released back into the corridor, Cat fell into Aldo's waiting arms. He was offering comfort and right now she needed it, she excused herself as his arms tightened around her and she buried her bright head into the wide angle of his shoulder.

Tomorrow, when she was over the shock of everything that had happened today, things would be very different. He would no longer be needed and she'd be able to stand on her own feet.

But when he brushed the tangle of hair away from her face and murmured, 'I've been talking to the senior nurse on duty. Preliminary tests show the attack was not too severe. There are more results to come in, of course, but we'll be able to talk to his consultant tomorrow and get a clearer picture,' she was not so sure, and clung to him weakly, needing his strength.

Only when they'd been shown to their hotel suite ten minutes later did Cat get a grip. Thankfully, there were two single beds, but even so the enforced intimacy made her spine go stiff.

She had told him she wanted a divorce and he had countered by telling her that she was his and he kept what was his, and had gone on to demonstrate just how effortlessly he could sublimate her will in his.

Sharing a room with him would be like going on a strict diet and having a plate of luxuriously wicked cream cakes dangled under your nose! she thought agitatedly.

A state of mind that markedly increased when he shrugged out of his jacket and loosened his tie just after a waiter had delivered a selection of sandwiches and an opened bottle of wine.

'Sit down and relax,' he told her gently, his bitter-chocolate eyes soft with compassion. 'We both need to eat and a glass of wine will help you sleep. The hospital has my mobile number. You will be called if you're needed, but I honestly think the possibility of that happening is very remote.'

Cat sank down onto one of the pair of brocade-covered chairs that flanked a low table, and when he gave her a glass of wine her hand shook. And her eyes were haunted as she watched him move about the room, unpacking for them both. Toiletries into the *en suite*; one of her nightdresses laid out on one of the beds. He had chosen her favourite, the pale aqua silk with the delicate creamy lace inserts, she noted with a violent stab of misery.

She remembered him buying it for her, and the matching wrap, when they were on that magical honeymoon in Portofino. His strong, lean hands had been so gentle as he'd taken it from the tissue wrappings, holding it in front of her and telling her huskily, 'I long to see you wearing this for me almost as much as I long to peel it off you.'

It seemed more than a lifetime away and the look of what she had only been able to describe as adoration in his dark eyes when she'd appeared in it later had been nothing more romantic and meaningful than the practised seducer's knack and the need to get an heir, she reminded herself forcefully.

She had believed that their marriage could work out beautifully. Now she knew differently, that it had never stood a chance.

'You must eat something,' Aldo instructed as he joined her and piled a selection of tiny triangular sandwiches on a plate and put it down on the table in front of her, before dropping fluidly into the other chair and lounging back, his long legs stretched out in front of him.

For a moment his eyes closed and Cat felt dreadful when she really looked at him and saw the lines of strain that bracketed his beautiful mouth, the shadows of fatigue that painted dark rings around his eyes.

He had had a dreadful day, too. Starting off with hearing his wife tell him she wanted a divorce. He might thoroughly deserve it, but at the same time it would have come as a shock. As far as he knew he would see his hopes of regaining those shares flying out of the window and that had to be a severe blow.

But, despite all that, if she tried from now until the next millennium she wouldn't be able to fault his care, his concern for her, or the ultra-efficient way he'd taken care of the travel arrangements.

Feeling guilty for so far only thinking of herself and what she had been going through since she'd seen Iolanda coming from his suite last night, and totally forgetting that he was flesh and blood, she managed gently, even though she felt her heart was breaking all over again, 'I'll eat if you will.'

'A done deal!' His heavy lashes lifted and his stunning eyes smiled into hers, the lines of fatigue washed away like magic as he sat upright, selected a sandwich and held it in his lean fingers. 'You first!'

His sinfully sexy eyes threw out a glinting challenge and Cat shivered with immediate response. She was looking at the man she had fallen so cataclysmically in love with and every last one of her senses reacted to him as shatteringly as they always did.

'I'm waiting—do you want me to die of starvation?' His mouth curved in the wicked smile that sent little electric sparks racing up and down her spine, and she answered with the first real smile she'd given him in what felt like ages. She took a bite and watched him pop the whole of his smoked-salmon-filled tiny triangle into his mouth with a feeling that she was shocked to analyse as melting tenderness.

She still really cared about him, she recognised with drenching dismay. In spite of what had happened she still cared deeply. She despaired of herself, she really did, she thought tetchily as she ate what she could and watched him polish off the remainder and help her to more wine, only sipping sparingly at his own barely half-filled glass.

She had to get a grip, keep firmly in mind what he was really like, protect herself from the insanity of loving him. And her voice was harsher, harder than

she'd intended, despite the supposedly mellowing in-
fluence of all that wine, when she told him, 'You
might as well go back to Italy tomorrow. I can manage on my own now.'

'Do you have to try to pick a fight?' Aldo's dark
brows clenched in a swift-as-lightning frown, his eyes
going bleak. 'I am your husband,' he reminded with
unnecessary forcefulness. 'My place is here with
you.'

'No.' Cat dragged air into her suddenly starving
lungs. For the whole period of their marriage he had
called all the shots while she had stayed wherever
she'd been pushed, dutifully trying to turn herself into
the type of wife she'd believed he'd wanted, always
there, willing, eager and responsive when he'd needed
her, keeping her misery and complaints to herself
when he took himself off to be with—as she now
knew—his mistress. 'No,' she enunciated more
clearly. 'I know—who better?—how busy you always
are. You don't have to stay on, because we don't have
a marriage left worth talking of.'

Cat put her empty glass down on the plate which
held the curling remains of her second, nibbled-at
sandwich and tried to stare him down. But his black
eyes ensnared her and made her mouth run dry.

'And I still don't know why you think that way,'
he countered with the chilling smoothness of polished
black ice. He got to his feet with the innate masculine
grace that was so typical of him. Then he stood over
her, incredibly still, his voice low and intense as he

warned, 'I don't want to discuss it. Now is not the time. For the time being we present a united front, for Domenico's sake. Remember his condition and behave yourself. We will discuss the subject fully at a time of my choosing. Now,' he gave her the benefit of a glacially polite smile, 'Will you use the bathroom first?'

Stumbling to her feet, Cat snatched her nightdress from the bed and locked herself in the bathroom. Her head was pounding with the strain of everything that had happened since Aldo had walked into the villa with the triumphant Iolanda.

And nothing had been settled about the divorce and it wouldn't be until Gramps was fully fit again. Aldo, as always, was right, she acknowledged with a seething fury that did her pounding head no good at all as she struggled out of her clothes.

They would have to pretend they were the perfect couple and she wasn't at all sure she could carry it off.

CHAPTER SIX

CAT woke feeling like a week-old corpse. As she forced her eyes open Aldo padded into her fuddled viewing range. He was wearing a towel slung rakishly around his narrow hips, his naked torso all sleek, power-packed muscles covered by silky golden skin.

Muttering a string of grumbling imprecations, Cat burrowed her head back into the pillow and pulled the sheet over her head, but with one lean hand Aldo twitched it away again and with the other placed a cup of steaming tea on the night table beside her lonely little bed.

'Drink this and you might feel more human.'

Annoyingly he sounded amused and, what was infinitely worse, he looked fresh as a daisy, full of his usual boundless energy as if this were another typical day which he could effortlessly sail through, his innate easy arrogance bending everything and everyone before him to his will.

While she felt as if she'd been buried for days and then dug up again. She hadn't slept until dawn, when she'd crashed into a sleep which had been peopled by spectacularly awful nightmares.

While he had instantly fallen into a deep and peaceful slumber, she had tossed and turned, wondering how her grandfather was doing, her ears standing to attention in case Aldo's mobile rang with bad news from the hospital, and all the time half expecting Aldo to wake, climb in with her and give her another lesson in his so easily achieved sexual mastery. Half dreading, half hoping. Needing him yet wishing he was half a world away.

Grumpily she hauled herself up against the pillows and tugged the sheet with a modest defiance up to her chin, ignoring the way he raised one mocking eyebrow before he turned and sauntered back to the bathroom, dropping the towel on the way.

Lordy, but he was so gorgeous! He exuded enough raw sexual charisma to turn the sanest woman silly. He would have no trouble at all when he came to choose a new wife. Someone who would stay besotted enough to look the other way when he strayed, his vast wealth providing a powerful anaesthetic.

Whoever she was, she was welcome to him. That type of sordid scenario wasn't for her, and the only thing she had to do to convince him that a divorce was the best idea since Creation was to assure him, no messing, that those wretched shares, the cause of all her present misery, would eventually belong to him.

The hot tea actually did help. She drank it in two thirsty gulps then scrambled off the bed and dived to the wardrobe to investigate the things Aldo had unpacked for her last night.

Selecting a pair of narrow dark grey trousers, a

silky white T-shirt and a light cotton jacket in dusky red, she draped them over her arm and plucked fresh underwear from one of the fitted drawers, listening for the sound of the shower to stop.

In happier times she would have joined him; now she just stood waiting, tense and simmeringly angry because she couldn't stop remembering just how it felt when his strong, clever hands soaped every inch of her body, every movement of his long fingers and curving palms intensely erotic.

Knowing what she did, she should be able to block all those memories from her mind, find him repulsive. But she was desperately weak where he was concerned, she acknowledged bitterly, thoroughly despising herself for the way her wretched body instinctively reacted to the very thought of him.

The opening of the bathroom door sent an electric jolt through her limbs to gather in a squirm-making burning knot deep inside her. He was freshly shaven, his dark hair clinging damply to his skull, his magnificent body entirely naked.

Her breath went, every inch of her skin tingling in that deeply regrettable response. With a small whimper of frustrated self-loathing she tore her eyes away from the cool, knowing mockery of his and dived past him, locking the door behind her. She wished she'd never met the self-serving, arrogant, unfaithful creature!

Cat took her time. She needed to find herself again, lose the lovelorn bundle of conflicting emotions she had become, the witless creature obsessed in every way there was by a man who would never love her, a man who would use his powerful sexual magnetism, his effortless charm to manipulate her for his own advantage.

Ready at last, she faced her reflection. The crinkly copper hair framed pale, serious features, the only colour the dark green of cold eyes, the defiant scarlet lipstick. Deliberately she compressed her mouth into a hard, narrow line, straightened her spine and walked through to the small sitting room.

Room Service had delivered breakfast. Aldo was sitting at the table beneath the window, pouring coffee into two cups. He barely glanced at her as she slid into the seat opposite, merely stated, 'Domenico had a good night and we may speak with his consultant at ten-thirty, after his visit.'

She accepted the cup and saucer. Her hands were steady, she approved. And said coolly, 'You pre-empted me. But thank you. I was going to phone the unit later.'

A barefaced lie! Too bound up in her own messy emotions, she'd unthinkingly left everything in Aldo's hands. But it would be for the last time, she thought, shaking her head as he offered her the toast rack, taking a ripe peach from the bowl in the centre of the beautifully laid table instead and slicing it into neatly precise portions on her white, gold-banded bone-china plate.

'You were right; we should present a united front

when we visit Gramps, at least for the time being,'
she conceded chillingly, unconsciously forming the
segments of fruit into a perfect circle. 'But away from
him we have to face reality. We can't pretend everything's normal.'

'Aren't you going to eat that? Or do you just want
to play with it?'

Detecting the thread of amusement, she raised cool
green eyes to him. He had finished eating and was
leaning back, one arm casually hooked over the back
of his chair. Seriously annoyed, Cat picked up her
fork and speared juicy fruit between her lips. A tiny
frown declared her perplexity. It wasn't like Aldo to
avoid hard facts, so why hadn't he taken her up on
her statement? It had been direct enough in all conscience.

Why didn't he want to face reality?

Lots of reasons!

Like gathering those shares back into his posses-
sion, like providing himself with an heir, like having
a dutiful doormat of a wife who was perfectly content
to be neglected while he enjoyed a life of hedonistic,
bachelor-type freedom!

Tossing her fork back down on the plate, she
reached for a linen napkin to wipe her mouth, did it,
then tossed it onto the mangled remains of her peach,
thrust her chair back from the table and stood up, all
in a series of tightly controlled movements.

'Face it,' she uttered, her voice low and clipped
with the effort of holding on to her temper. 'I want

out, and you know it. Yet you won't discuss it. You're so damned arrogant you don't even want to know why!'

'But I know why,' he countered mildly. But his eyes were strangely bleak as he, too, got to his feet. 'As I recall, you said you didn't like our marriage.' Two paces brought him to within a few inches of her space and despite all her good intentions her body began to overheat, her heartbeat quickening. 'And to the best of my recollection,' the dancing golden lights that now gleamed at her from those bitter-chocolate eyes did what they always did—melted her back-bone—and the now sexily intimate tone he employed made her mouth go dry and her pulses race, 'I was able to prove that you liked it very much indeed.'

Sex. He was talking about sex. About his ability to seduce her out of her senses. There was no point in denying it and she wasn't stupid enough to try. The point was, 'There is more to marriage than having sex together—when you happen to be around.'

'Yes? Then why don't you show me? I am quick to learn, *bella mia*. But before you complete my education, we could consolidate on what we both know you *do* like.'

He lifted his hand, the movement so slow she had time to move if she wanted to. She knew what was coming, but he mesmerised her, and the atmosphere was so thick and heavy she could taste it. It sizzled on her tongue, spread through her veins and pooled hotly between her thighs.

A tiny, yearning whimper was forced from her throat as that hand finally made contact and slid beneath her jacket to touch the sensitive peak of her breast, linger for a tantalising moment and then, just as she was spilling into that hot, curving palm, withdrew and clamped around the back of her head, long fingers tangling in the tumbling curls as he drew her towards him.

His kiss was almost brutal, hot and possessive, taking her breath away, pushing her headlong into a losing battle for self-control. And only when she began to respond with fevered abandonment did he break it, black eyes glimmering down into pools of hazy green shame as he mocked, 'You want me, *cara*. I can prove it just like that.' Lean fingers snapped cynically. 'I have already told you that I will listen to your complaints at a more suitable time, so until then stop having tantrums and get ready to leave. We don't want to miss Domenico's consultant.'

'I hate you!' Cat whispered passionately as they stood in the small visitors' waiting room. She'd been seething furiously with bitter resentment since the humiliating aftermath following the primitive domination of that kiss, and it just had to come out before the consultant appeared.

'Calm yourself.' It was the voice of authority that had doubtlessly quelled unfortunate underlings who had failed to live up to his high expectations but Cat wasn't to be classed as an underling and her eyes narrowed further, spitting green fire in his direction.

He was wearing a dark grey suit in some beautifully structured, silky-sheened fabric, a pale grey shirt and a paler tie. He looked cool, remote, capable of controlling any situation.

Abruptly, Cat swung round to stare out of the single window that overlooked a dreary vista of roof tops. He was going to have to learn that he was no longer her puppet master. She had cut the strings.

Her rigid spine turned towards him, she heard the door open, heard his greeting. And turned back, her eyes fixed on the consultant, hanging on every word he said.

Ten minutes later her knees were sagging with relief. The attack had been minor, with no damage done. After a few more days of observation her grandfather would be able to go home. He would be given advice on diet and a mild exercise regime, and medication to lower his blood pressure.

'That's great news!' she breathed happily, her hatred for her husband temporarily forgotten as they walked the few paces to the unit and waited while the door was unlocked. She had been so desperately afraid that her grandfather wouldn't recover or, if he did, that he would have to spend the rest of his life as a semi-invalid. Despite his age, he had always been an active man. He would hate the restraints of chronic illness.

'Keep that smile on your face and you won't upset

Domenico,' Aldo advised with patronising smoothness as they were admitted. Cat totally ignored him
and swung towards the bed in the far corner.

'Gramps—you're looking so much better!' He was,
too, she thought as she hugged him gently. He had
lost that frightening grey colour, and although he was
still on a monitor he'd been taken off the drip and the
oxygen.

'I am a fraud,' Domenico admitted as Aldo brought
two chairs to the bedside. 'I am told I escaped lightly,
for which I am thankful, but I have dragged you both
here unnecessarily and I feel bad about that. I know
how busy you are, Aldo, my boy.' His brown eyes
glistened with weak tears. 'And you, my poor
Caterina, dragging you here and worrying you over
what turns out to be nothing but a warning when you
have had such trouble of your own—'

'Hush!' Cat took his hand, horribly aware that he
was upsetting himself, the news of her miscarriage
still recent in his mind, his longed-for great-
grandchild a hope dashed. 'I am fully recovered now,
truly.' Her fingers tightened around his. 'And as for
my busy husband—' the saccharine smile she turned
in his direction would fool her grandfather but it
wouldn't fool Aldo, not in a million years, and it
wasn't intended to '—now we know you will be fine
as long as you take proper care he can get back into
harness and I shall stay here and help Bonnie look
after you until you're really back on your feet again.

It will be a holiday for me, too, I promise you. So I don't want any arguments.'

'I have missed you,' he admitted gruffly. He returned the pressure of her fingers, his eyes misting over until a broad smile made them dance with all his old vigour as he turned to face Aldo. 'Caterina was always the stubborn one. Even as a toddler and learning to talk, she refused to call me Nonno and insisted on that ugly Gramps. So I won't waste my breath trying to make her change her mind, so long as you don't mind a short separation, my boy?'

He wouldn't have to mind, would he? Cat thought on a wave of heady triumph. He didn't have a leg to stand on when faced with Gramps's obvious pleasure at the thought of her being with him for the duration of his recuperation. And the short separation would become a long one, lasting a lifetime.

But, 'No separation will be required,' Aldo slid in smoothly.

Cat shot him a spearing glance. Her skin prickled in warning. He looked like a cat who had just swallowed a very fat canary!

He smiled at her, a slow, dangerous smile that chilled her to the bone. 'When Caterina became pregnant I started to reschedule my working life,' he explained to her grandfather. 'It necessitated much hard work. Then, sadly, our baby was lost and I used her recuperation to increase my efforts to visit and appraise every aspect of my business interests, to hand the reins over to employees who had earned my trust.

I freed myself up during the period of her recovery so that I could devote a great deal more of my time to my wife and, hopefully, my future family. My time is now largely my own. Happily I can be here too.'

Cat gulped away the sudden and unwelcome lump in her throat. Had he really been doing that? For her? If he'd bothered to explain all those absences she would have understood!

Then, Gullible idiot! she scolded herself. All that flannel was just to pull the wool over the older man's eyes, make him think what a wonderful, considerate and caring husband he was. When those absences had really been his opportunity to skive off with his vile mistress.

Once she was safely pregnant he had been free to swan off; unsafely unpregnant he'd had to return to do his duty all over again when the time was right, she reminded herself bitterly, and when she tuned in to the conversation again she went cold with horror.

'I have been thinking,' Aldo, lounging back, thoroughly at ease, was saying. 'When you get your doctor's go-ahead, Domenico, you might like to return to Italy with us. I know my parents are anxious to get to know you better. You are the missing part of our family; we all want to have you with us. And Caterina and I would love to give you a long, relaxing holiday. Bonnie must accompany you; that goes without saying. Apart from anything else I'm sure she has earned a rest. What do you say?'

If she'd been asked that question she would have

answered that he was a manipulative monster, Cat bristled silently, trying to keep her face from contorting with the need to strangle him.

That was why he'd been asking questions about Bonnie's situation, she recognised acidly, not because he'd wanted to take her mind off what had lain ahead at that time. He was trapping her with her love for her grandfather for his own despicable and mercenary ends.

Before he could reply she gave her grandfather's hand a final squeeze and got to her feet. 'We must go. We mustn't tire you.' How she managed to keep her voice on an even keel, a smile on her face, she would never know. She bent over to kiss him, promising to visit again in the evening, asking if he needed anything, filling the few minutes with soothing chatter until she was out in the silent corridor again, Aldo a smugly self-satisfied presence right behind her.

She turned to face him, wanting to slap his bland and blameless, too beautiful face. 'What did you do that for?' she threw at him, the need for play-acting over now they were outside the unit, the need to lash out at him positively explosive.

He put his hands on her shoulders and turned her round to face the lifts at the end of the corridor, his expression still smack-worthily bland, as if he'd never played a devious hand in his life. 'Do what?'

'You know what!' Cat's voice rose to a shriek of fury but she clamped her mouth shut as the doors of one of the lifts hissed open to reveal two nurses and a cleaner with an industrial polisher coming out. Red-faced with embarrassment, fully deserving the half-humorous, half-curious looks she'd earned herself and with Aldo's hand firmly in the small of her back, she allowed herself to be propelled forwards into the empty waiting lift, and only when the doors had closed them into the small, downward-travelling space did she let rip.

'Why stay on when you know I want you to go?'

'Domenico's peace of mind?'

'Rubbish!' she spluttered rudely. 'And then, to cap it all, you invite him to stay with us in Italy when you know full well I won't be there!'

'Silenzio!' Hard hands reached for her, pulled her into close, intimate contact and silenced her with his mouth. He plundered her lips with a passion so raw and hungry it made her dizzy, breathless and out of it. Small fists pummelled at those wide, dominating shoulders but the battle was lost, and she knew it as his tongue probed with deepening intimacy and her legs went from under her.

She hated what he could do to her, what he could make her, yet her whole being craved him. She was hooked and she'd never get her rehabilitation under way if she gave in, just melted, every time he touched her!

The whimpers of protest had turned to ragged little gasps of pleasure, when a high-pitched giggle and an appreciative male 'Atta boy!' brought her crashing back to her senses.

The lift had come to rest, the doors sliding open. Doing her best to ignore their enthusiastic audience, Cat unravelled herself from where she'd got herself twined all over Aldo and shot out into the crowded hospital foyer, her face scarlet, her self-esteem somewhere under the floor.

And her infuriating husband was just behind her. She could feel his lazy, sardonic smile all the way down her spine.

CHAPTER SEVEN

'OH—I'M that glad to see you!'

Bonnie was waiting at the open door of the former farmhouse, wreathed in the kind of smile that threatened to split her pleasantly round and wrinkled face into two quite separate pieces.

While Aldo was fetching their luggage from the boot of the hired saloon Cat returned the housekeeper's enthusiastic bear-hug. As he'd checked them out of the hotel after their visit to the hospital Cat had phoned to warn Bonnie of their imminent arrival. His suggestion, but she'd more than readily concurred.

If she couldn't talk him into going back to Italy, and it was now obvious that he wouldn't be budged— short of her having him kidnapped—then she'd be better off back in her own surroundings. She'd be more in control. Well, wouldn't she?

'And I'm that relieved your grandad's going to be all right I don't rightly know where to put myself!' the housekeeper cried. 'And your old flat isn't suitable, not for a couple, so I've made up the bed in the guest room. Much better than you staying in a nasty hotel, and I've put a batch of scones in the oven! You don't get good home cooking in hotels!'

Cat found a weary smile, said, 'Lovely,' and

couldn't be bothered to impart the information that the hotel had been very far from nasty and she couldn't eat a thing to save her life.

'*Buongiorno,* Bonnie—how nice to see you again, especially now the news of Domenico is so good. I do hope we're not imposing?'

The charm of Aldo's smile as he joined them, the smooth silk of his voice, set Bonnie fluttering, her face going decidedly pink, Cat noted with a quiver of disgust. He could charm his way out of hell itself, she decided morosely as Bonnie burbled eagerly, 'Not a bit of it, *signor*! Imposing, indeed! I'll be glad of the company. Now, let me take those up for you and then I'll make coffee.'

She reached for the cases but Aldo said warmly, 'Coffee would be most welcome, Bonnie, if you will share it with us? And I'll carry our luggage up. Caterina will tell me where we're to sleep. You've been through a rough time over the last day or two and we refuse to put you to any extra trouble.'

'This way,' Cat threw out and headed for the stairs. Any more of this and poor old Bonnie would be a simpering heap on the floor!

She had always viewed the guest room as being gloomy but this morning it looked positively sombre. Dense cloud cover had hidden the earlier late-August sunshine, making the panelled room look dark and heavy, and the carved oak four-poster with its muted tapestry hangings looked wildly uninviting.

'There's a bed in the dressing room.' Cat indicated

the connecting door in the carved oak panelling with a sharp dip of her bright head, letting him know she had no intention of sleeping with him, tonight or any other night for that matter. 'No *en suite*, I'm afraid, but there's a bathroom next door down the corridor. I'll unpack my stuff later. And we're going to have to discuss the divorce; you can't keep sweeping it under the carpet and pretending it isn't an issue,' she warned bleakly.

She swung on her heels and was saved from whatever he might have come back at her with by the ringing of his mobile, and she left as he was fishing the slim instrument from the breast pocket of his jacket and went down to have coffee with Bonnie.

Doing her best to force down a scone so as not to disappoint the woman who had been like a second surrogate mother to her for as long as she could remember, Cat listened to a much dramatised account of the trauma of Gramps's collapse and, pouring herself a second cup of coffee, eventually butted in with, 'You were wonderful; I dread to think what might have happened if you hadn't been here and kept your head—and you must be tired out. So why don't we have a simple salad for lunch? I'll throw one together. It's too hot and sticky to bother with anything cooked. And I won't be in for supper; I'll get something in town after I've been to visit Gramps. I don't know about my husband...' How that word stuck in her throat! 'You'll have to ask him.'

As if on cue, Aldo strode into the old-fashioned

farmhouse kitchen. Cat immediately shot to her feet. As Bonnie got up to make a fresh pot of coffee for him Cat told her in passing, 'I'll go and see what Dan's got to offer in the way of salad stuff,' and swept out, sparing Aldo the merest glance.

But that glance was enough to tell her that the phone call he'd received hadn't pleased him. Hoping it was a cry for help from the manager of one or other of his various business ventures, something only he could deal with, in person, this minute if not sooner, she left the house through the door in the utility room.

The midday heat was oppressive, but nevertheless Cat was glad of the breathing space. Her brain was apt to misbehave when she was around Aldo—she was either yelling at him or falling into his arms, and neither was in the least bit sensible.

Believing that a gentle amble around the garden, on familiar home territory, would help to settle her, she wandered along grassy paths between billowing herbacious borders glowing with rich, late-summer colour and through the clipped hornbeam tunnel. Coming at last to the round garden, she stared at the arching sprays of tiny white roses that surrounded the central sundial and her eyes filled with wretched tears.

It wasn't working. She felt like a displaced person. She was here in an English garden, part of her former life, part of her happy childhood, but her heart was stubbornly back in Tuscany. Maybe she had more Italian genes than she'd reckoned on.

Or was her heart really locked back in those few

short months when she'd truly believed the man she loved could and would begin to really care for her?

That kind of sloppy, sentimental line of thinking didn't deserve headroom—events had proved her wrong, with a vengeance—so she scrubbed her eyes with the back of her hand and headed purposefully on and found Dan in the potting shed.

He came in for a few hours each day, always had done for as long as she could remember, and he regarded the garden and everything in it as his own personal, jealously guarded property.

So she had to ask very politely and with a suitable note of deference, 'May I help myself to salad stuff?' If she'd gone to the kitchen garden and picked what she needed Dan would have sulked for days on end.

'You're back, then.' The elderly man's hands worked steadily on, placing salvia cuttings in pots of compost. ''Bout an hour ago Bonnie come down and told me your grandad's going to be all right; she didn't say nothing 'bout salads.'

'We've only just decided,' Cat explained, trying not to grin at his curmudgeonly tone. 'It's far too hot to cook lunch.'

'We're in for a storm.' It was as near as he would get to agreeing with anyone. About anything. The compost in the last pot tapped down to his satisfaction, he straightened his bent shoulders. 'I'll cut what's ready to be cut and take it up to the house. Should have asked sooner. I'll likely as not get a right soaking while I'm about it. So will you, if you don't hop it.'

Taking her dismissal gracefully, Cat stepped out into the humid air. Dan was a grumbler, he was famous for it, but what he didn't know about growing things wasn't worth knowing. Which was why everyone put up with him.

But he had a nice side, too, a side not many people got to see. He might dislike his fellow human beings, but watch him handle a seedling, or hear him give an encouraging pep talk to an ailing clematis, and he was like a tender father with a precious newborn!

The encounter had taken her mind off other things, cheered her in a funny sort of way, and far from taking Dan's advice she left the main garden and headed for the deep belt of trees that bordered the property on three sides.

There was a maze of narrow bark paths and they all eventually led to a secluded summer house. She would sit there and reflect on the way her life was going and get herself calm and collected before she had to face Aldo again and make him accept the fact that their doomed and unworkable marriage was over, and that taking her to bed to prove a point was unworthy.

And downright wicked, she grouched to herself as she felt her face go pink when she recalled how sinfully easily he had been able to do just that.

The first violent clap of thunder, sounding ominously close, had her momentarily frozen to the spot, and the almost simultaneous appearance of Aldo, heading her way from a different direction, had her practically leaping out of her skin.

Altogether she was in no fit state to voice any objections when he caught her hand and pulled her in the direction he had come from, and he sounded as if he was almost enjoying this, as if the storm dovetailed with his mood when he said, 'I just passed a round hut arrangement. We can sit this out.'

The open-fronted summer house—Cat recognised his description as the first heavy drops of rain penetrated the leaf canopy. They made it just before the heavens opened, penning them in with a solid curtain of water. He had taken time to change into narrow-fitting, worn jeans and a darker blue T-shirt and he looked absolutely spectacular, his staggeringly attractive lean features lit up by a blinding flash of lightning, the spiky black lashes adding a *frisson* of mystery to his dark, unreadable eyes.

'Alone at last, no interruptions, nowhere to go. Time to talk?' She heard the dry mockery in his voice and shivered. Cat knew exactly what he meant. This, at last, was the right time and place.

She had many precious, happy memories of this place. Alone or with her friends from school. The summer house had doubled as an enchanted castle, an ogre's cave, a fort to be defended from marauding Red Indians, a place for lavish picnics provided by Bonnie or, as she'd reached her teens, simply a place to sit alone and daydream.

It seemed a shame to spoil all those wonderful memories by adding a vile one that would smother and choke all the others. But, she reminded herself tartly, this was no time for sentimentality.

Feeling cold and strangely leaden, Cat sat in the middle of the bench seat that curved around the outer wall, stingingly aware of the suddenly intense way he was looking at her. Waiting.

She stared fixedly at the wall of rain.

Swallowing uncomfortably, her pulses racing as she took the plunge, she dragged in a deep breath and reminded him quietly, 'Neither of us pretended to be in love with each other when we married.'

She had to be fair about that. He had never been less than honest on that score. And for her part she had kept silent about the way she felt because he'd told her that he didn't want the emotional upheaval that would crash around his head if he married a woman who was in love with him because he would be unable to return it, and he didn't want that kind of complication.

'I could accept that,' she admitted heavily.

Accept it because, naïvely, she had really believed she could change it.

And now for the words that would force him to understand why their marriage was dead and couldn't be healed by the gift of a pretty jewel or his spectacularly passionate lovemaking. It would be an ending. Final. Her throat closed over the words. She felt empty.

Hugging her arms tightly around her body, as if she was defending herself against something unspeakably dreadful, she forced it out in a voice that was tense in the effort to hold her feelings back. 'As your wife I expected—deserved—your respect and fidelity. You gave me neither. As soon as you knew I was pregnant, you took off with your mistress.'

She heard the sharp tug of his breath and slid in quickly because she knew her carefully contained control would shatter into a million screaming pieces if he tried to lie his way out of this—and, God help her, she might let herself be fooled into believing him! 'Do you remember that dinner party you gave soon after our honeymoon?'

He didn't answer that; she hadn't expected him to. This wasn't a normal conversation. She tried to look relaxed and made a conscious effort to fold her hands loosely together in her lap.

He settled himself on the bench at her side but made no attempt to touch her, and she couldn't bear to look at him although she could feel those bitter-chocolate eyes on her stoically expressionless features.

She couldn't afford to betray herself, let him know how much she was hurting inside. She had to keep all those rioting emotions firmly at bay, pretend she was talking to a stranger about something not particularly important. Cool, matter-of-fact statements delivered without bitterness or anger was the way to play this.

'Iolanda told me she was your mistress. She was quite civilised about it, of course, and explained that such an arrangement was considered normal and acceptable by men such as yourself. Men who marry for dynastic reasons.'

The quality of his watchfulness had changed, hardened. She had felt it as soon as she'd mentioned the other woman's name. He'd been caught out and naturally enough he didn't like it and was going on the defensive. So be it. She sighed softly, even though she hadn't meant to.

'I didn't find it at all acceptable. I guess I'm not sophisticated enough to take that sort of behaviour in my stride. But I didn't believe her, not then, even though you started to treat me like a house guest in daylight and at night time like a whore.

'Then things really changed. Everything began to slot together. I got pregnant. You moved to another room. You stayed away for days on end. You'd done your duty as you saw it. Then the miscarriage. I got hidden away…'

Her voice had wavered; she swallowed sharply, annoyed with herself for allowing even a hint of emotion to show through, and retrieved her former even tone. 'And while I was kicking my heels in luxurious isolation you and Iolanda had a couple of months together—until it was time for you to come back and try to get me pregnant again.'

She pulled in a deep breath. Her fingers, she noted, were knotted tightly together, a sure sign of inner tension. She straightened them out, kept them clasped loosely together in her lap again and wondered why he was just sitting there as if he'd been turned to stone, saying nothing.

And told him, 'Even then I wasn't absolutely sure. I had no real proof that she'd been telling the truth until that night. I couldn't sleep. It was the early hours of the morning by the time I decided that I had to ask you for the truth. She was coming from your room. She left me in no possible doubt about what you'd both been doing. As your wife, I believe I deserved more respect, better treatment than that.'

She had done it, Cat congratulated herself bitterly. He wouldn't have a clue how deeply and permanently he'd hurt her, how she'd bear the scars for years to come. She had, at least, salvaged her pride. But the victory was a great, hollow ache inside her and she wanted to vent all the pent-up pain and emotion in his direction but knew she couldn't do that and be able to walk away from this marriage with her head high.

There was a truly stark silence. Nothing but the now distant rumble of thunder, the rain hitting the canopy of the trees.

It was desperately unnerving. Cat had fully expected him to try to wriggle out of this. After all, those rogue shares were at stake—or so he believed. So why wasn't he telling her she'd got it wrong? Repeating the excuses he'd given to her grandfather for his long neglect of her, telling her that Iolanda had been lying, promising to punish his blabbermouth mistress by giving her the sack?

After all, willing mistresses would be ten a penny in his rarefied stratosphere. Wives who came packaged with a bunch of coveted shares weren't all that thick on the ground.

Cat ventured a sidelong glance. His bronzed skin was abnormally pale, his jaw rock-hard, and there was not a shred of warmth in those furiously narrowed black eyes. As if the turning of her head had sparked off some terrible rage inside him, he rose to his feet, shot her a look of compressed loathing and stalked out into the rain, his dark head high and proud, the atmosphere around him positively smouldering.

Pressing her fingers against her trembling mouth, Cat stopped herself from venting a cry of anguish. She started to shiver. Apart from lust she had just witnessed the first gut-wrenchingly real emotion Aldo had ever experienced for her.

Anger. Plain, old-fashioned, explosive anger.

In his eyes, she translated, she hadn't measured up. It was as simple as that. She was neither docile and cowed enough, nor sophisticated and blasé enough to shut her eyes to his extra-marital activities. She had made a fuss, demanded a divorce. That sort of reaction didn't fit with his idea of a marriage of convenience.

And the telling fact that he hadn't tried to shoot her accusations out of the water, convince her that Iolanda had been lying her socks off, invent a credible excuse for the wretched woman's presence in his bedroom, only emphasised the truth. He wasn't going to lie about his affair with Iolanda. She, Cat, simply wasn't worth the indignity of his having to do that.

And the swamping waves of desolation that engulfed her as she wrapped her arms around her trembling body just went to show what an abject fool she was.

She hadn't known it before, but she knew it now. In her heart of hearts she had secretly hoped that he would have moved heaven and earth to convince her that he'd never had an unfaithful thought in his head, much less acted on it.

Half an hour later Cat walked slowly back to the house through what was now a steady drizzle. Slipping in through the utility room, she found Bonnie in the kitchen.

'Oh, there you are! Dan told me he'd warned you a storm was coming.' She eyed Cat's damp clothes, the copper curls that clung to her skull, with an expression more reminiscent of sorrow than of anger. 'At least you didn't get as drenched as the *signor*. He's gone up to change. You'd better do the same while I see to lunch.'

'Bonnie—' Cat thrust her own troubles to one side; the older woman looked tired out, wisps of grey hair had escaped from her normally neatly tight bun and her shoulders drooped '—I'll do it. Why don't you go to your room and catch up on some rest?' she suggested softly. 'You must be bushed. I'll bring you a cup of tea in a couple of hours or so.'

'Well...' Bonnie looked doubtful, but did confess, 'I wouldn't mind putting my feet up for half an hour. I haven't been able to sleep for the worry.'

'There's nothing to worry about now; Gramps is going to be fine,' Cat affirmed gently. She put her arm round the housekeeper's sagging shoulders and walked her to the door. 'So you can catch up on all that lost sleep with a quiet mind.'

She would be needed here for several weeks, if not months, Cat recognised as she watched Bonnie slowly head for her room. The housekeeper was no longer young and Gramps would need lots of TLC when he came home. Aldo wouldn't want to stay around for an indefinite period and he wouldn't be able to insist she return to Italy, not under these circumstances.

Not that he would want to do either, she reminded herself dully as she headed slowly up to the guest room. The look he'd turned on her as he'd stalked out of the summer house left her in no doubt that he actually hated her.

As if the breakdown of their marriage was entirely her fault!

The knot of dread in the pit of her stomach tightened unbearably as she approached the guest room. Her heart was thumping as she pushed on the door, her head spinning dizzily at the thought of having to face him, encounter that anger head-on.

She had had enough, she thought wildly, pressing

the tips of her fingers against her throbbing temples. She couldn't cope with any more. The loss of her baby, Aldo's infidelity, the shock of Gramps's heart attack—she couldn't hope to handle the rank unfairness of being made to feel responsible for the breakdown of her marriage on top of all that!

The bedroom was empty, she noted with a strange sense of anticlimax, nothing to show signs of anyone having been here except for her unpacked suitcase at the foot of the looming four-poster.

And then he walked through the connecting door and her heart stood still for long, breath-depriving moments then raced on, tumbling about inside her chest. He had changed into a dark, beautifully cut business suit. He looked intimidatingly handsome, intimidatingly cold. He looked through her.

Cat's head started to spin. There was a roaring sound in her ears and her throat went so tight she felt she was being strangled by unseen, vicious hands. She swayed on legs that were suddenly the consistency of jelly, put out a hand seeking support and, finding nothing but thin air, she staggered.

Aldo gave an impatient hiss. *'Perfetto!'* he grated on a note of deep, sarcastic exasperation as he dropped the case he was carrying and covered the distance between them in three loping strides. Strong arms caught her, holding her upright. 'Trust a woman to pick her moment!' he gritted in a fierce undertone as he lifted her bodily and placed her with not too much reverence on the bed.

Hands on his lean hips, he stared down at her with impatient eyes. 'I have the jet on standby, I have to drive the hired car back to Birmingham and you pick this moment to stage a collapse! *Dio!* Just look at you!'

Cat's eyes were swimming with weak tears, so she couldn't be sure, but she thought she saw his black eyes suddenly soften with compassion. She only knew she didn't want him to go. Which was nothing if not perverse of her, she knew that much, but she couldn't do anything about the panicky feeling of loss that came out of nowhere and utterly overwhelmed her.

'Are you leaving?' Of course he was. But she had to be sure. Maybe she'd misheard him.

'Naturally,' he said flatly, his eyes turning to flint. 'It is what you say you want. And, since you are unable to give me what I need from this marriage, it is what I want also.'

What he needed! Her blessing on his extra-marital activities! A sob choked her and the tears escaped, pouring down her ashen cheeks.

Frowning down at her, he muttered something that sounded very rude and ground out, 'You need attention. I will ask Bonnie to come to you.'

'No!' Cat tried to get herself upright, failed in the attempt, and flopped weakly back against the pillows. 'Bonnie's resting,' she muttered, ashamed of her body's wimpish descent into feebleness. 'She's worn out. And I'm fine.'

'You are far from fine,' he uttered in a voice so

cold it sent shivers down her spine, his eyes narrowing as they swept over her. Then he made a sound like a man who had just received a hefty punch in the stomach. '*Dio!* What am I to do with you?'

He sat on the edge of the bed and took her icy hands between his, gently rubbing warmth back into them. A warmth that spread its seductive tendrils all through her body. There was a rough note in his voice as he murmured, 'Events have overtaken you. That is what has happened. One way and another, you've been through a lot, been so brave and strong, and now it has all caught up with you. It is to be expected.'

Brave and strong? Cat's eyes went wide as she tugged her hands from his. If she'd had any courage, any strength at all, she would have refused to marry him in the first place! She would have put the painful pangs of unrequited love down to experience and got right on with her life!

'Don't be stubborn,' Aldo chided gruffly, recapturing her hands and exerting a brief gentle pressure before lifting them and looping her arms around the back of his neck. 'Listen to your body; it is telling you that you need to rest and relax, take time out.'

It was telling her no such thing! Cat thought on a shudder of despair. It was telling her she still wanted this man, loved him in spite of everything.

She must have done something unforgivable in a previous existence to warrant this kind of punishment, she decided bleakly. And as her eyes drank in the masculine magic of his hard bone structure, the harsh lines around that long, sensual mouth that told of internal strain, the dark, dark eyes, her limp fingers took on a life of their own and slid eagerly into the warm luxury of his hair.

Briefly, his eyes swept down to fasten on her parted, tremulous lips and then he said tightly, 'Hang on to me; I will lift you. Then you will be able to get out of your wet clothes more easily.'

In one smooth movement he had lifted her to her feet, his hands clamped on either side of her waist. Her arms still looped tightly around his neck, she could feel his body heat through the damp layer of her clothing, inhale the fresh and tangy, enticing male scent of him and see every individual lash that so lushly framed those spectacular bitter-chocolate eyes.

A hopeless little cry was wrung from her as she pressed her weary body closer to his. Fully aware that she was being ridiculous, she could do nothing about the driving need to hold him for just one more time.

Their marriage was over and, for all she knew, she would never see him again, so was one final brief moment of closeness really too much to ask, if only for the sake of the sadness they had both shared when she'd lost the little life they had created together?

'Don't!' he commanded with harsh warning as he swiftly released her hands from their stranglehold around his neck. 'Don't cling. You may be hungry for the only thing I could ever give you but I have lost my appetite. Get out of those wet clothes,' he instructed tersely as she raised stricken green eyes to his. 'Or do I have to do it for you? And if you're really that incapable then I shall phone for a doctor before I go.'

'Shut up!' she snapped nastily, the import of what he'd been saying hitting her brain like a sledgehammer. Did the conceited so-and-so really think she'd been begging for sex? When all she'd wanted—silly, misguided, sentimental fool that she obviously was—was to hold him for one last time, mark their final parting with softness instead of bitterness. 'Just go; I don't need you hanging around like a wet weekend,' she blistered unfairly. 'I can look after myself.'

'You have made a swift recovery,' Aldo commented with withering dryness. He picked up his abandoned suitcase and glanced at the watch that graced his flat, bronzed wrist. 'I am running short of time. But before I go,' he said with flat finality, his cold black eyes making a swift inventory of her face and body, as if checking whether she was fit to be left on her own, 'I advise you to keep the news of our impending divorce from your grandfather, at least until he has made a full recovery. I will handle everything from my end. I'll phone now and then to check on his progress.'

And left. Just like that.

Left her staring at the space where he had been, harbouring the first thought, which was that she would never see him again. And then the second, which was that he obviously wasn't afraid of her laying claim to a great chunk of his assets and losing, as he imagined he would, those wretched shares. That package of losses had been the sole reason for that previous statement when he'd vowed that he didn't let go of what was his, and that included her.

Somewhere along the line something had changed. He wanted rid of her at any price!

She had no idea how long she'd been standing there when the sound of the telephone in the hallway below brought her out of her miserable trance-like state.

Bad news from the hospital about Gramps? Oh, no, dear heaven, don't let it be that, she howled inside her head as she flew down the stairs. And her voice came out in a breathless rush as she lifted the receiver and gave the number.

'Pass me on to Aldo, please.'

Iolanda's tinkly voice! That was all she darn well needed!

'I was expecting him to return my earlier call. I know how difficult things are for him right now but it's personal and important. I've tried his mobile, but it's switched off.'

'Get lost!' Cat growled and replaced the receiver with a satisfying crash, then dropped to the floor and cried as if she would never stop.

CHAPTER EIGHT

ALDO would be arriving in less than an hour! She didn't know how she was going to be able to handle it!

As Cat glanced at her bedside clock her stomach leapt. She felt drained and distinctly nauseous again and she flopped down on the four-poster, sitting right on the edge, staring at her feet while she waited for the unpleasant sensations to subside.

His phone call, two days ago, had come as a shock. Not the call itself, because over the past three months he'd phoned fairly regularly for the sake of appearances, but because of what he'd said.

He always asked for information on her grandfather's progress then left the rest of the not very long conversation down to her. Idle babbling into an uninterested silence that had broken her heart all over again, but necessary if the pretence of a stable marriage was to be kept up for the benefit of Gramps's sharp ears at this end of the line.

But this time he'd said, 'Expect me in two days. Around seven on Wednesday evening. It's been over three months and Domenico is now strong enough to be told about the divorce. This situation can't go on any longer and it's best if we tell him together.

Presenting a united and civilised front will hopefully take the edge off what will come as an unpleasant shock.'

His voice had been so hard and impersonal. Just thinking about it set up a shivery reaction all over her body, made her battered heart ache. Trying to block the way he'd sounded out of her aching mind, she shot to her feet and crossed the room to draw the heavy brocade curtains to shut out the dark, mid-December evening.

She should be changing, not sitting around feeling sorry for herself. Gramps had said, 'Run along and pretty-up. You haven't seen Aldo for months—far too long in my opinion. So wear something glamorous and remind him of what he's been missing!'

Glamorous was out. All her designer gear was back in Italy. And even if it weren't, her mood tended more towards sackcloth and ashes. Gramps didn't know it yet, but Aldo wouldn't have missed her at all. He was as anxious for the divorce as she was, but for entirely different reasons.

Plucking a garment at random out of the wardrobe and fresh underwear from one of the drawers, she carried them to the bathroom and ran hot water into the huge, claw-footed Edwardian tub. Perhaps a long soak would calm her nerves, although she seriously doubted it.

As always, Aldo was right, she thought frustratedly as she lowered herself into the scented water. The time had come.

In the early days of his convalescence Gramps had unquestioningly accepted the fiction of the sudden business crisis that had necessitated Aldo's immediate return to Italy. But as he'd grown stronger and fitter and late summer had turned into late autumn she was sure he was harbouring suspicions.

'There's really no need for you to stay on,' he'd stated briskly as she'd accompanied him on his pre-scribed morning walk a couple of weeks ago. 'Don't think I'm not grateful for all you've done. I am. Truly. Hiring Mrs Peterson from the village to do the clean-ing and laundry was a brilliant idea of yours, too. I'm a selfish old man, Caterina. I hadn't stopped to think that Bonnie's getting older as well. So, now we're all settled—thanks to you—and I'm feeling better than I have done in years, it's time you got back to your husband.'

Her excuses for staying on had been pretty thin but he'd had no option but to swallow them, particularly the one about her need to tag along when he had his appointment with his consultant, although he had pro-tested that he didn't need a nursemaid.

The appointment had been and gone and he'd been given a clean bill of health, and the approach of the Christmas season had brought more probing ques-tions. Would Aldo be joining them here, or would she be returning to Italy? And as for the holiday Aldo had promised himself and Bonnie, well, he was hugely looking forward to it. Some time in the coming spring would be nice.

So yes, it was time.

But she wished she'd taken the matter into her own hands before now, not left it to Aldo to decide when the time was right. As always, it seemed, he was the one to take the lead, leaving her to tag along behind.

Many times over the past few weeks the news of the breakdown of her marriage had hovered on the tip of her tongue. But always she'd held back. Something had stopped her from actually spelling the situation out. Not only because she had known it would really upset her grandfather—her reluctance to actually say the words and make it all official went deeper than that. She was sure it did, but for the life of her couldn't exactly say why.

And now she could hit herself for the lost opportunities. It could all have been done and dusted by now and Aldo wouldn't be on his way here to break the news in person. She didn't want to have to see him again. It would bring her far too much pain.

Belatedly aware of the remorseless passage of time, Cat dressed in a hurry and only fully realised when she checked herself in the mirror back in her bedroom that the dress she'd plucked so haphazardly from the wardrobe was the one she'd worn at their first, fatal meeting.

Too late to change now. In any case, what did it matter? she asked herself snappishly, taking extra care as she applied her make-up because her hands were shaking so badly. He probably wouldn't remember.

Why should he? He had only been interested in her grandfather's business proposition, not in her.

He had never been interested in her, she reminded herself grittily. And when he'd seduced her, that very first night, he'd probably shut his eyes and pretended she was Iolanda!

Cursing herself roundly for letting her nerves get her into this hyper state, she scowled at herself in the mirror, tucking straying strands of curly copper hair behind her ears, turned sideways and surreptitiously viewed her body profile.

There was just the smallest hint of a bulge, but nothing anyone would notice. Not yet. Just a soft roundness where before her tummy had been concave. Her heart turned to warm treacle and a tiny smile erased the former tension from her features for a few short moments as she placed a near-reverent hand over the tiny new life.

Her secret. Her baby.

History wouldn't repeat itself, she vowed fiercely. It would not! She would carry this baby to full term. She was taking good care of herself and her GP had told her, during her last sneaked visit, that everything was fine. The first three months were the tricky ones and they were already behind her.

Everything would be fine.

The only decision she had to make was whether or not she would ever tell Aldo he had a son or daughter. But that could wait; she'd think about the implications at some later date.

Feeling more reassured and in charge of her life than she'd felt since she'd received the shock phone call that had sent her into a state bordering on panic, she cast one last probing look at her reflection then went down to see if Bonnie, who was cooking up a storm, needed help in the kitchen.

'That was a truly splendid meal!' Aldo complimented Bonnie as the last crumb of her famous apple pie disappeared. 'No, don't get up,' he instructed warmly as the elderly housekeeper, dimpling with pleasure at the praise, made to rise from the table. 'Caterina and I will clear away and make the coffee.'

They had eaten in the library, the cosy book-lined room, the open log fire a good choice if relaxation was on the menu.

But Cat couldn't relax; she felt like a too tightly strung-up chicken just waiting to be roasted. Since his arrival Aldo had been behaving normally—too normally. She didn't understand why. Surely it would be better to get everything out in the open straight away. Why prolong the painful charade?

Fortunately, she'd heard the crunch of his hired car's wheels on the gravel before anyone else had. She'd been listening for the first sounds of his arrival until her ears had ached.

She'd wanted to warn him that Bonnie had insisted on cooking the fatted calf in his honour and that if he wanted to avoid having to sit through several courses, feeling awkward because their bombshell was still unexploded, then they'd better say their piece right now and then he could leave.

As he'd walked in out of the darkness, wearing that beautiful cashmere coat, his lean face was taut, his sensual mouth compressed. And he was carrying a soft leather suitcase, not a small one, either, and her warning fled out of her head, replaced by, 'Surely you don't intend staying here overnight!'

The narrowed eyes that swept over her tense body were dark with something she couldn't put a name to and she heard the rough intake of his breath, yet his response of, 'I don't intend sleeping in the potting shed, if that's what you have in mind,' was flat and dry.

'Use your brain, can't you?' she hissed, appalled by the scenario that presented itself. 'If you hang around until the morning Gramps will make us sit up all night while he busts a gut trying to get us to change our minds! Do you really want that?'

'Not particularly.' The skin over his harshly sculpted cheekbones tightened. 'Which is why I came prepared to stay. It will give us the opportunity to talk things out, in private, before we hit him with the divorce.'

Things? What things? Cat hopped from one foot to the other in agitation as he put down the case and removed his coat. Then it hit her. Of course! The size of the settlement he was afraid her lawyers would demand from his.

As she opened her mouth to reassure the avaricious

streak in him that wouldn't want to part with a single lire, tell him that she wanted nothing from him, the words were snatched right out of her mouth by Bonnie's, 'I thought I heard something! Did you have a good journey, *signor*?'

Grinding her teeth with frustration at the lost opportunity that surely would have had Aldo smartly revising his plans, Cat gave up and went to the kitchen on leaden legs, leaving Bonnie to show him through to the library, where the round tripod table was already laid for a lavish supper and Gramps would be waiting.

Now, as she followed Aldo through to the kitchen, clutching a pile of dishes while he carried the piled-up plates, Cat saw her chance.

Tell him she wanted nothing from him and would sign any papers to that effect, then they could break their news and he could disappear. Where to, exactly, was his problem. She couldn't bear to have him around much longer. In spite of what he'd done he still had the power to turn her will to water, to make her want him, love him, reducing her self-discipline to thin air.

And if he stayed overnight Gramps would expect them to share the same room. There was always the dressing room, of course, but even so—

But again the housekeeper put paid to any hopes of her making the speech that would have him showing a clean pair of heels!

'No man does dishes while I have breath in my

body!' she carolled, swooping on Aldo's pile of plates. 'Domenico has been so looking forward to seeing you, *signor*; go through and keep him company and I will make coffee.' She was already rinsing plates at the sink, prior to stacking them in the dishwasher. 'Domenico and I will not have any. We'll retire and leave you two young things together.'

Since when had Bonnie used her employer's first name? She'd obviously been at the wine bottle, Cat thought sourly, uncomfortably remembering the quirk of Aldo's darkly defined brow when she'd refused wine herself.

He couldn't suspect, of course he couldn't, Cat told herself staunchly as Bonnie shooed him out of the kitchen. Her tummy was only a little rounder and the only real pointer to her condition was the way her breasts had grown, well, quite a lot fuller, actually.

Hoping he wouldn't have noticed that interesting fact, even though every time she'd looked up from her barely touched meal she had found those dark, unreadable eyes on her, she plugged in the kettle to make coffee and tried to close her ears to Bonnie's chatter, which largely centred on how ecstatic she must be to have her so handsome husband with her again.

'So there you are—I was just coming to see if you'd got lost!' Gramps huffed when Cat finally arrived with the loaded coffee tray. She began to force a smile so that he wouldn't guess that she'd had to steel herself to come back here at all but it faded as

Aldo rose to take the tray from her, one dark brow sardonically raised, his mouth flat and ungiving.

'I was just telling Aldo that it was high time he came over here and fetched you, since you wouldn't budge no matter how hard I tried to push you.' He turned to the younger man. 'She seems to think she's got to molly-coddle me and all the time she's been pining for you! Picks at her food and looks half-dead every morning. And if that's not pining, I don't know what is.'

Cat could have throttled him—he made her so furious! As far as Aldo understood it, pining away for him would be the last thing she would be doing. She had been the one to insist on a divorce. Therefore— Oh, it didn't bear thinking about...

She swung herself away from the pair of them, sitting in the winged armchair, facing the fire, cutting out her view of the quizzical golden light in the depths of Aldo's darkly speculative eyes.

'If I've been looking frayed round the edges,' she muttered from the depths of the chair, 'then you can put it down to having to run round you, making sure you keep to the regime of diet and exercise you've been given; left to your own devices, you'd be pigging out on cream cakes and fry-ups.'

'Touché.'

Cat heard the grunt of humour in the old man's voice as Aldo came to stand in front of her, holding out a coffee-cup. Raising her eyes to him, she silently pleaded, Tell him now! and he must have been able to read her mind because he simply shook his head and her decision to take the matter into her own hands and tell him herself, put an end to this senseless charade, was only half-formulated when her grandfather ruffled her hair, said a gruff 'Goodnight, see you both in the morning', and disappeared.

The ensuing silence, broken only by the crackle of the fire and the moaning of the cold winter wind around the old house, sizzled with tension. Then Aldo made his move and Cat's hands clenched into tight fists in her lap.

'So.' He dropped into the chair on the opposite side of the brightly crackling fire. He rested his elbows on the arms and steepled his hands, the pads of his long fingers touching his mouth. 'Where to begin?'

His endless legs were stretched out, the soft fabric of the narrowly cut trousers of his dark business suit moulding tautly muscled thighs. Too intent on trying to fight the ravaging effect the wretch always had on her to conjure up a sensible reply, Cat glared into the dancing flames, denying herself the self-defeating and painful satisfaction of looking at him at all.

'Nothing to say? You have changed!' he commented drily. 'Too ashamed of your behaviour?'

She pulled in a sharp, sudden and desperately painful breath. 'What did you say?' Stung by the utterly unforgivable unfairness of that remark, she bristled straight back at him, having to glue herself to the chair to stop herself from jumping up and strangling him. 'You are the one who should be ashamed!'

'In some respects, yes,' he drawled levelly. 'Which is partly why I am here now. You accused me of unspeakable things,' he added in a tone that told her that the dominant Italian male expected any woman he had elevated to the position of his wife should have had enough sense to hold her tongue, close her eyes to his philandering and be grateful for the honour of bearing his name.

Cat's green eyes went dark and narrow as she glared at him and pointed out, 'You didn't deny them.'

'Why should I demean myself?' he asked with quelling cool. 'You angered me almost beyond my ability to contain myself. I bitterly resented your low opinion of me. What you accused me of made me out to be worse than an animal. So I decided there and then that if you wanted a divorce, you could have it. If you couldn't give me what I wanted from our marriage—your trust—then I wanted no part of it either.'

Her browline knotted in a scowl, Cat recognised his devious male tactics. He was turning the tables, putting all the guilt onto her. Well, he wasn't going to get away with it!

She made a conscious effort to smooth her forehead and manufacture a chilling little smile, and came smartly back with, 'I almost forgot—silly me!—but shortly after you left me the lovely Iolanda phoned. She was expecting you to call back on some important and personal matter, apparently. Though I expect you've managed to sort it out; you have been back with her for over three months.'

For a few short moments his shatteringly gorgeous features were blank, as if he didn't know what she was talking about, and then he dismissed edgily, 'Oh, that. She had phoned me earlier, saying there was some problem back at Head Office. I told her to deal with it; that was what she was paid handsomely to do.

'Which brings me back to what I had started to explain before I got sidetracked. After I got Iolanda to confess to everything she'd said to you I dismissed her immediately. Even so, it took me some time to recover from the injury you'd dealt me. Then I began to see how you might have come to believe her. You were still fragile, your hormones all over the place, after that miscarriage. You would have been easy prey for a malicious woman who was deeply jealous of you. Though how she could possibly imagine that I would ever have thought of her as anything other than a first-rate assistant, I can't think.'

'You're saying she *wasn't* your mistress?' Cat slotted in between trying to grasp what he was saying, wanting so very badly to believe him, yet not quite daring to.

'I am saying you should have been able to trust me.' He gave her a dark, condemning look. 'And I'm saying that, finally, I can forgive that lack in you, at that time, due to the prevailing circumstances. My being away so much can't have helped your state of mind.'

Was he implying she'd gone loopy? Did he have that much gall?

Cat sat very upright as he got to his feet with the fluid grace that always made her breath catch in her throat and her knees go weak. She hated him for his ability to do that to her, loathed him for the way he was trying to lay all the blame on her!

She registered the slight clink of the neck of the wine bottle against glass and unthinkingly shook her head when he handed one of the glasses to her, missing the slight tightening of his mouth as he replaced it on the dinner table and took up a looming, straddle-legged position in front of the hearth.

'I came here with the intention of giving you moral support when we told Domenico of our plan to divorce. But when I saw you again—my frame of mind had calmed sufficiently to make me wonder if I should ask you if we could try to make something of our marriage.' He targeted her muddled mind with the deadly accuracy of a cruise missile.

And it took long moments of his dark, unwavering, questioning scrutiny for her to emerge from the chaos of his making and come back with a cynical, 'I see. You'd rather put up with me than miss out on my grandfather's shares and have to shell out a considerable sum by way of a settlement.'

'Don't be so ridiculous!' he grated with formidable

fury, the cool he had maintained throughout this disappearing at the speed of light.

He slammed his wineglass down on a side-table and swung round to glare down at her. 'Before I even laid eyes on you, you idiot woman, Domenico told me that he had changed his will and that his shares would eventually come back to me, to the family, where they belonged, irrespective of whether we married or not. He also told me that you knew of this.

'I tried to change his mind because I considered that he was behaving like a barbarian, but he was adamant. Apparently, he felt ashamed for having cut loose all that time ago, taking his share of the profits without doing a stroke of work for the family business, and he wanted to make reparation. All this,' he blistered forcefully, 'because I had responded to his idea of a marriage of convenience with the doubts that any modern young woman would give such an archaic concept any headroom at all. He said he'd put the right kind of pressure on you; you would either have nothing, or everything. And when it comes to that, when have I ever been less than generous to you? A divorce settlement would not cause me to lose a wink of sleep.'

Stark incomprehension tightened his savagely beautiful bone structure. 'Is there any sin you won't happily accuse me of? *Madonna mia*—I am not a greedy man. I don't ask for your love, only for your trust, which you are patently unable to give! Do you have any idea at all how much I resent all this? How it makes what we did have together tawdry and worthless?'

Cat's brain was spinning out of control as she tried to put what he'd been saying into some kind of logical order. Who was really to blame for what had happened? She could no longer be sure. Was that what this was all about? The steady stream of counter-accusations, designed to make her feel humble and guilty? And why on earth did he want to keep their marriage intact if—?

'But I have changed my mind; you will not be consulted on the subject.' He interrupted her frantic thought processes with a voice that was now as cool as ice. 'There is no question of a divorce. You are pregnant.'

Filled with horror, Cat felt her body shrink into the chair. How could he possibly know? It was the last thing she needed. She hadn't yet decided whether to eventually let him know he was to become a father or not. Was even this to be taken out of her hands?

'What do you mean?' she managed with what felt like the last feeble breath in her body.

'Pregnant? How to explain it?' He made an insulting pretence of sinking into deep thought. 'Having conceived. With child. Will that do?' he asked with a lazy drawl that made her heart clench with a greedy need to slap his handsome, arrogant face.

'I know what it means—don't treat me like a fool!' She snatched at what little composure she had left.

'What I meant was, why would you think I'm pregnant?'

'Oh, this and that.' He rocked on his heels, thrusting his hands into his trouser pockets. 'I remember how it was for you for the two months you carried our first baby. The bouts of nausea in the early mornings, your commendable insistence on avoiding all alcohol. And you have gained weight.'

'Eating too much.' She tried to dismiss that with an airiness that didn't quite come off and solidified into a lump of dismay in her chest when he reminded her,

'According to Domenico you merely pick at your food, so that won't wash.' His following and utterly scathing, 'With your history you should be constantly monitored. I don't suppose you've even bothered to see your local GP.'

'I have!' Stung by the implication that she was uncaring enough to neglect any aspect of the welfare of the precious child she was carrying, she sprang to her feet, her eyes blazing in the parchment pallor of her face. 'I have!' she repeated furiously. 'And everything's just fine!'

The swift flash of triumph in the depths of those stunning eyes had her shaking like a leaf. She had just unthinkingly given him the truth, all the leverage he needed.

The hard curving of his sensual mouth made her knees wobble and confirmed her opinion even before he said with derisive contempt, 'I will not do you the dishonour of suggesting the child you carry is not mine. And as its father I insist we stay married. My child deserves both mother and father. And be warned, if you persist in starting divorce proceedings I will move heaven and earth to have custody.'

Tears fell then, sliding down her cheeks. And she was too numb with the shock of what he'd said to avoid the hand he raised to gently brush the moisture away. 'Go to bed,' he advised softly. 'I won't disturb you when I come up. Tomorrow we will talk again.'

He dropped a light kiss on her forehead, a kiss that actually shocked her because she had expected nothing remotely caring from him. 'Go now. Sleep.' And she went, heavily, like a very old woman. She didn't know what she felt. Just that, as before, she was a captive wife.

Held captive in the beginning by her hope that he would grow to love her as she loved him.

Now she was to be held captive by their coming child.

CHAPTER NINE

WRIGGLING irritably, Cat made yet another determined effort to get comfortable, but the Jacobean
four-poster bed seemed to have sprouted lumpy rocks
and jagged hollows all over the place.

By her reckoning several hours must have passed
since, with her head buried under the elaborately
quilted bed cover, she'd heard Aldo walk quietly
through and firmly close the dressing-room door behind him.

He was only a matter of yards away, separated by
a panelling wall and an unlocked door. If she listened
hard, would she hear him breathing?

Jerkily, she pushed at the quilt and soft woollen
blankets. She was much too hot. She couldn't seem
to breathe properly, either. And her brain wouldn't be
quiet and let her get to sleep. Hazy plans that had
hovered on the periphery of her mind ever since she'd
learned of her pregnancy coalesced into startlingly
vivid clarity now that it was all much too late.

She could have moved back into the flat above her
workshop, created a comfy nest for herself and her
baby, taken up her abandoned career. At least she
could have designed and made the pieces and farmed
them out for someone else to sell. Supported herself

and her child—no domineering input from a husband who merely put up with her—and hopefully saved enough so that when the time came and she had to move out she could afford to rent half-decent premises somewhere.

But that wouldn't have been fair on either Aldo or their child, one of the conflicting, argumentative and sleep-denying voices that had taken up residence in her head reminded her starkly.

To deny him knowledge of his child would have been despicably selfish, she had to admit, she thought guiltily. If she lived to be a million years old she could never forget how ecstatic he'd been when after missing a period she'd done a home test, secretly had it confirmed and was able to announce that they were having a baby. Or his stark grief when she'd lost the little life they'd both held so precious at ten weeks.

She sat up amid the muddle of tangled bed covers and dragged her fingers through her already wildly rumpled hair. She'd had no right to think, even for one moment, that she could keep their baby's existence from him. As usual, he was right; a child needed both parents. And they could rub along fairly amicably, provided he didn't replace Iolanda with someone of her ilk.

So had he definitely not had an affair with Iolanda, then? That question still actually needed answering. All that anger at her lack of the trust that he said was so important to him could have been the natural reaction of a man who was stuffed full of arrogant

Italian pride. He would grind anyone who didn't consider him to be perfect to dust beneath his heel.

And yet—there were other aspects of what he'd said to her that needed clarifying. Aspects which, now she'd had time to properly think about them, offered a newly emerging green shoot of hope.

There was no time like the present. Get the clarification she needed and maybe, just maybe, she'd be able to get some sleep.

Slipping her feet to the floor, with her heart hammering away at the base of her throat, she dragged the quilt off the bed and covered her naked body and headed for the connecting door.

As she pushed on the smooth wood she cringed inside and she felt dizzy enough to lose her balance and fall in a heap. Was this really the right thing to do? Or would it be better to wait until the morning?

But there had been too many occasions when she had stubbornly held her tongue, her pride not allowing her to ask questions.

Too many occasions when he'd shut her out, made her feel surplus to requirements. If there was to be any hope of making their marriage work on any level at all she had to know if the tiny bubble of hope was worth harbouring and cosseting or whether a few terse words from him would prick it and reduce it to nothing.

Whatever, she needed answers, didn't she? And she needed them now!

With her breath lodged beneath her breast bone and

her legs feeling distinctly shaky she pushed the door fully open. Aldo hadn't bothered to close the curtains and moonlight fell directly onto the narrow bed.

He seemed to be soundly sleeping. Cat moved tentatively forward, the quilt dragging behind her, conscious that she was holding her breath.

He was facing her, moonlight emphasising the planes and angles of his stunningly gorgeous features, heightening the contrast between his dark hair, the thick twin crescents of his lashes and the olive tones of his skin.

One arm lay over the top of the down-filled duvet, exposing a hard, muscled shoulder. Cat took a deep breath, reached out and gently shook it, and caught in another breath, more ragged than the first, as the contact between her skin and his had the all-too-familiar electrifying effect.

'You want something?' He sounded fully alert, his black eyes immediately opening, pinning her with lancing intensity.

Cat withdrew her hand as if she'd been scalded and backed off a pace. He must have been awake all the time, watching her tentative approach through the thick screen of his black lashes, waiting while she plucked up the courage to lean over and touch him.

He was proving himself to be a dab hand at putting her at a disadvantage, she thought, not knowing whether to laugh or to cry. She moistened her dry-as-desert-sand lips, swallowed the strange lump in her throat and answered, 'To talk?' and it came out as a quavery question and nothing at all like the imperative she had intended.

'Sure. Why not?' he drawled lazily, hoisting himself up against the pillows and shifting over. 'Sit down—unless you'd like to climb in with me. It's a bit narrow, but we'd manage.'

Manage what? Cat wondered hysterically, her eyes glued to his hard, muscular torso. To have sex? They'd always managed that, no problem!

'I'll sit,' she said in a prim, tight voice and hoped the cold wash of moonlight would bleach out the hectic colour that was making every inch of her skin burn. She lowered herself gingerly to the very edge of the bed, her legs getting tangled in the heavy folds of the smothering quilt.

'This is not a social visit, I take it?'

'It's not funny,' she chided huffily. The undertone of amusement she'd detected in his smooth drawl wasn't making this any easier.

'Perhaps not. But it could be fun.'

'Don't!'

'Don't what?'

'Be so flippant.'

She watched his eyes narrow, felt the mental distance he now put between them, and when he asked coldly, 'Then tell me how I'm supposed to react when the woman who has literally accused me of being a monster and tried to hide the fact that I am to be a father pays a visit in the small hours,' she shuddered as a wall of ice washed right the way down her spine.

This wasn't going to plan. She could almost hear the air hissing out of that brave little bubble of hope. He was making her out to be a really vile person, someone that any man in his right mind wouldn't want to know.

Averting her eyes, shrinking deeper into the smothering quilt, she finally got out what she'd found the courage to come and ask. 'Why did you marry me?'

One long, aching silence. Then, on a snap that sounded suspiciously defensive, 'You know why.'

'No, I only thought I did.' Cat ventured a sidelong glance at him. His arms were folded high over his impressive chest, his tough, shadowed jawline clenched. He looked very far from relaxed.

But this was too important a point to be merely shrugged aside; it could affect the whole of the rest of their lives together.

So she elaborated quietly, 'I thought,' she stressed gently, 'that you'd looked at what was on offer—the property and shares that would come to me eventually—and decided you were on to a good thing. You did tell me on that very first meeting of ours,' she reminded, in case he happened to have forgotten, 'that a man in your position looked for a wife who would bring something of substance to the marriage, that family honour and sound financial sense demanded it.'

She turned to face him fully, grabbing at the quilt that was sliding off one shoulder, and stated firmly, 'But I was wrong, wasn't I? Because before you so much as set eyes on me you knew you would get those shares, as well as everything else, because Gramps had already told you. You had no need to marry me to get what you wanted. You knew that, so why did you?'

Disconcerted wasn't in it. His narrowed, moody eyes flicked to her and away again and the skin tightened over his slashing cheekbones.

Cat shuffled just a little bit closer and, her skin dampening with the tension of wondering if maybe she'd got her wires crossed, pressed home this rare advantage. 'And apparently it wasn't because you'd taken one look at me and fallen madly in love. You're not into that sort of delusory nonsense, or so you were at pains to point out. Or did you change your mind on that score?'

She was actually coming out with it and asking if maybe, just maybe, he'd married her for love, and a million butterflies were whirling around inside her tummy as she waited for his response.

It came almost immediately. 'I took one look at you and wanted you naked and in my bed!' he sliced at her in a charged undertone. 'I wanted you like hell! Satisfied? Is that what you wanted to know?' he demanded rawly. 'You know exactly what I'm talking about because that night your eyes told me you felt the need, too.'

Dark colour stained his taut features as he told her grimly, 'I agreed to visit Domenico when he eventually contacted me after the deaths of his sister and his wife. It was obvious that he wanted to heal the rift with my side of the family and I guess I felt sorry for him and wanted to facilitate that. As for that pro- posed arranged marriage, well, I wrote that off as an old man's pipedream. But when I saw you I knew I had to have you whenever I wanted you, and if that meant agreeing to what I'd considered—right up until that moment—Domenico's lunatic idea of an ar- ranged marriage, then so be it.'

'So you seduced me.' Cat's voice was flat. She hadn't liked the sound of what he'd said. He certainly hadn't given the answer she'd so desperately hoped for. That the sexual chemistry between them had been immediate and explosive wasn't in any doubt, but she had wanted—hoped—he might have confessed to something deeper.

With a harsh sigh Aldo admitted, 'I am not proud of myself for that. For the first time in my life my hormones got the better of my common sense,' he tossed out disgustedly. 'I behaved like a callow youth pumped full of testosterone.'

'Yet that night was the most wonderful experience of my life,' Cat said softly, gently reassuring, because it actually physically hurt her to hear him putting him- self down. 'And it got better.'

'So it did.' He shot her an underbrow look, then, his hard mouth curling with a mixture of contempt and derision, 'Until you believed Iolanda's lies.'

Cat's soft mouth dropped open. He had finally ad- mitted the foul woman had lied! That was good enough for her! She wanted to fling her arms around him, kiss him until he didn't have an ounce of breath left in his body.

Instead she contained herself with quivering difficulty and asked sympathetically, 'How did the lying harpy get herself into your room that night? What sort of excuse did she make up?'

His dark eyes found hers, held for long, sizzling moments before he huffed in a deep breath, expelled it on a slow sigh and asked gently, 'Does that remark mean you finally get to trust me?'

Cat nodded violently, too choked to utter a single word, despising herself for letting the malicious lies of a jealous woman poison their relationship. Her emerald eyes welled with emotional tears as he reached out and took her hand.

Then he shifted on the pillows and his face lit up with the type of grin that sent her heart soaring into orbit. 'I was already deeply annoyed with the wretched woman! For the way she'd spoken to you, the way she invited herself to stay—an invitation she would have had to take right back again if you hadn't jumped in and endorsed it.

'Then you'd tipped me out of your bedroom and the planned happy reunion with my wife was turning into a farce and I couldn't sleep for wanting you and wondering what was going wrong, and telling myself to give you more time because you obviously weren't over the loss of our baby, and in walks my personal assistant, as good as naked, bleating about being restless, having a headache. I told her to get the hell out, grabbed a pack of painkillers from the night-table drawer and threw them at her. I also told her to be ready to leave first thing in the morning.'

He lifted her hand to his lips and placed a kiss in the palm, not taking his eyes off her widening, watery gaze. 'I had no idea you'd seen her—how could I have if you didn't tell me? And as there's no way I'm going to let you turn your back on our marriage you're going to have to air any grievances—real or imagined—that might crop up in the future. Promise me?'

She nodded, the tears spilling over. She'd been such a fool, she castigated herself. If she hadn't bottled everything up inside her then none of this trauma would have happened. Their marriage hadn't been perfect and maybe she'd been greedy to expect that he would love her as she loved him. Which reminded her...

'Don't cry,' Aldo murmured gruffly, knocking her thought processes off line. 'There's nothing to be sad about. I forgive you,' he tacked on with an air of magnanimity that made Cat suppress an inner giggle and love him even more, warts and all. 'And now that's all out of the way, are we back on track?' he asked with what she could only describe as a suspiciously wolfish smile. 'If we are, I have no objections to you joining me, provided you get rid of whatever it is you're bundled up in. There's not room for it and us in here.'

The invitation was too tempting. Cat tried to resist for all of a full half-second then joyfully gave in, uninhibitedly dropping the quilt from around her naked body and sliding in beside him, every inch of her skin quivering helplessly as her body fused into the lean, hard length of his.

'There're just one or two more things.' She persisted in following her interrupted line of thought while she could still speak, arching her spine hedonistically as his arms came around her, fitting her more intimately against him, his mouth finding the tender hollow at the base of her throat while she struggled to find the words to complete what she'd started.

'If you hadn't tricked me into admitting I was pregnant, would you still have wanted to stay married to me?'

'But of course.' A soft line of kisses marked the delicate arch of her collar-bone. 'Why do you think I refused to listen when you kept rabbiting on about a divorce, and immediately changed my mind about giving you what you wanted when I saw you again and realised my damaged pride wasn't really worth sacrificing our marriage for? Discovering you were carrying my child gave me all the leverage I needed.'

Aldo hoisted himself up on one elbow, his eyes simmering down into hers, level and serious. 'The big question is,' with one gentle hand he brushed the tangled copper hair away from her forehead, 'we both made mistakes and put our marriage at risk. For my part, I've already forgotten them because I know you do now trust me. But are you happy to remain as my wife? No more talk of divorce?'

'Not unless you seriously annoy me!' She reached up and touched the unsmiling line of his mouth with delicate fingertips, but he didn't respond and she whispered, sincerity making her voice shake, 'Of course I want to stay with you! I wouldn't be here in this bed with you if I didn't.'

That verbal reminder of the way their naked bodies were practically welded together in the confined space sent each of her nerve-ends haywire. With a tiny gasp she fitted her hips into the cradle of his and wound her arms around his neck, dragging his head down, her full breasts pressed urgently against the broad expanse of his chest.

Cat felt his body shudder in response, but his mouth was a tight line still as she whispered against it, 'You said you weren't a greedy man. You didn't expect love in our marriage, but you did expect trust. Did that mean you wanted love, but weren't greedy enough to ask for it?'

Aldo's big body tensed. He unwound her hands from around his neck and dropped them. Hauling himself up against the pillows, he stared into space. He might have been turned to stone.

Cat held her breath, her heated flesh going cold. Had she got everything so very wrong?

She couldn't breathe for the dread of it until he said in a tone of deep aggravation, 'I gave myself away with that, didn't I just? *Madonna mia*—of course I wanted you to love me! I told myself I was marrying you because you were the first woman I'd ever wanted to own, to possess in every way possible. But, looking at you on our wedding day, I knew I felt something very different. Lust was a very small part of it. Love had crept up on me and hit me when I wasn't looking!'

'Why didn't you tell me?' Cat kept her voice suitably demure because the poor darling was obviously having a hard time right now and this wasn't the most sensitive moment to vent the ecstatic, triumphant shout that was bubbling up inside her.

'And make myself look ridiculous?' he questioned on a note of the male's savage impatience with the female's dim-wittedness. 'As far as you were concerned, you'd married me because otherwise you faced a rocky future. With no inheritance to count on to take your one-woman business into viability, you'd have to sink or swim on your own. So you took the sensible option. And let's face it, you knew the sex was good. Was I really expected to make a fool of myself and confess I was insanely in love with you?'

Cat could have made quite a few serious and highly voluble objections to that portrait of a woman who would sell her body for a life of idle luxury. And the bonus of great sex. But she wasn't going to argue the toss with him about anything. Not any more.

Instead she scrambled as upright as she could get without falling off the narrow bed, looked him straight in the eye and stated very firmly, 'I crashed

headlong in love with you that first night. I knew I
wanted to spend the rest of my life with you, loving
you. You'd already said you didn't believe in the condition—' her wide mouth softened into a tender, understanding smile as she registered his involuntary
flinch '—so I crossed my fingers and hoped you'd
eventually change your mind about that chunk of
masculine idiocy.' She leaned forward and put her
lips against his shell-shocked mouth. 'I promise you,
I'd have married you if you'd had no prospects and
nothing but the clothes you stood up in.'

And then it happened. The golden gleam came
back to those bitter-chocolate eyes, making the silvery
wash of moonlight that surrounded them pale into insignificance. His strong arms wrapped lovingly
around her as with one fluidly sexy movement he laid
her back against the pillows and took her mouth with
a kiss that was so achingly tender it made her want
to weep with the total beauty of it.

She was weak with wanting him, with the insistent
pulsing heat between her thighs. He was so beautiful,
so hard, so sleek, so perfectly packaged. And he loved
her, her heart sang ecstatically as she wrapped her
legs around the hair-roughened length and strength of
his and felt the needy, greedy response of him as his
kiss deepened passionately and her body writhed fe-
verishly against him.

'No! *Mi amore*, no!' With a harsh, driven cry, he
put her gently away from him. 'What am I doing to
you?' he uttered on a note of bitter self-castigation.

'We must remember our baby. Last time I was level-headed and unselfish and removed myself from temptation. Your gynaecologist had explained to me that sex was possible during the first three critical months but that it must not be—I think the word he used was excessive.'

He ran an unsteady yet infinitely loving hand from her temple to her jawline. 'I had no option but to move to another bedroom because our lovemaking has always been…excessive, *mia cara.*' He sighed with draining regret. 'You should return to your bed before I forget my good intentions. Yes?'

'No.' Cat trailed seductive fingers over hard, muscled flesh, following the line of crisp hair from his chest to the base of his sex, muting his raw groan of driven denial with her soft lips. 'The three months are already safely behind us and who knows how unexcessive we can be if we don't try? I promise you it will be all right,' she murmured as he shuddered in sharp response. 'If we take it nice and slowly.'

Nice was too insipid a word to describe his languorous and inevitable capitulation. It was something beyond heaven, Cat thought deliriously as Aldo covered her body with slow, luxurious, reverential kisses, and when he finally could contain himself no longer he entered her with slow, measured strokes that only intensified the almost unbearable pleasure, drawing it out until she exploded cataclysmically beneath him and afterwards, when their mingled sighs of draining satisfaction left them with breath to speak, he said proudly, 'I managed it, *mi amore*! I was not excessive and I think it was the most beautiful thing I have ever experienced. For you too, yes?'

'Oh, yes,' she breathed, still monumentally shaken by the whole loving experience, melting into boneless satiation as he enfolded her into his arms.

'How often I had wanted to hold you after making love with you. I never did quite dare because I knew that if I did I would end up revealing my true feelings for you.'

'Which are?' Cat mumbled through a deliciously sleepy smile, snuggling her head against his broad, accommodating chest.

'That I love you more than my life.' He nuzzled his cheek against the top of her head. 'And every day I will remind you of that, until you get sick of hearing it,' he warned.

Which will be never, Cat thought blissfully as she drifted off to sleep.

CHAPTER TEN

'YOU'RE spoiling me,' Cat said, smiling blearily through a tangle of copper curls as Aldo brought her late breakfast in bed.

'Just getting some practice in.' He gave her his wide, nerve-tingling grin as he settled the tray on her knees. 'I'm going to spoil you for the rest of my life, so get used to it.'

'Sounds good to me!'

Cat shifted slightly to make room for him to sit on the side of the narrow bed. As always, her gorgeous husband looked fantastic, good enough to eat, his lean, powerful body clad in a soft black cashmere sweater and a pair of beautifully cut stone-coloured chinos. Smooth, sophisticated, yet possessing a rawly lethal masculine sexuality and that air of natural command that set him head and shoulders above any other man she'd ever met and turned women's heads wherever he went.

And he was hers, and he loved her, he really loved her—life couldn't get any better!

'Is that all right?' He indicated the contents of the tray with a slight inclination of his glossy dark head. 'Bonnie and Domenico are out for a walk and the last I saw of the cleaning lady she was taking a flask of tea down to Dan in the greenhouse. There was no one around to ask what you managed to eat in the morning. Last time, I remember, you threw up at the sight of anything edible.'

Cat dimpled at the totally unprecedented note of hesitancy in her normally self-assured husband's voice. 'You've thought of everything,' she assured him, then burst out laughing when a flush of mortification spread over his unfairly handsome features as they surveyed his offerings together.

A glass of fruit juice, another of milk and yet another of bottled water. Two cups, a pot of coffee, a tiny pot of herbal tea, a single slice of toast and a boiled egg complete with a quilted cosy. A peeled and segmented orange in a glass dish.

Their eyes met and he joined her laughter. 'I might as well have added the kitchen sink,' he admitted as she wiped her eyes with the backs of her fingers, poured coffee for him and the herbal tea for herself.

'I haven't actually thrown up at all this time,' she confessed as she bit into the dry toast. 'I've sometimes felt a bit queasy in the mornings, and a bit down in the dumps—but that was more to do with the misery of facing another day, knowing everything had gone so dreadfully wrong for us.'

'I'm sorry, *mi amore*.' He reached out a hand and ran the backs of his fingers down the side of her face, regret deepening his husky voice. 'I should have been with you. I should have stayed and made sure we

thrashed the whole sorry subject out instead of leaving you alone, feeling betrayed and ill.'

'Not ill,' Cat assured him, melting under the sober
scrutiny of his darkly regretful eyes. 'Physically, I've
been feeling fine. Fit as a fiddle and as happy as a
lark now that we're together again and everything's
been sorted out.'

Well, not exactly everything, but the rest could wait
until later, she decided as he said, watching her with
eyes that were drenched with love again as she sliced
the top off her egg, 'You may feel fine, but we're
going to have to get you properly checked out. Does
Domenico know you're pregnant?'

'No, I haven't told anyone. And I have had a
check-up. I did tell you.'

Aldo brushed aside her input. 'Thoroughly checked
by your gynaecologist back in Florence. He knows
your history better than anyone.'

The authoritarian note was well and truly back in
evidence and Cat said meekly, 'Anything you say,'
and meant it because he had to be as concerned as
she was about their baby's continued safety, even
though, fingers crossed, she was pretty sure everything was going to be OK.

But later, as she was dressing, having sent Aldo
packing because time was racing by and his insistence
on running her bath, and soaping her all over, not to
mention patting every inch of her body dry, then
anointing every last pore of her skin with perfumed

body oil, had delayed things considerably, she wasn't quite so sure.

Sometimes the sheer terror of losing this baby came out of nowhere and sent her into a state of jibbering panic, despite the reassurances of the obstetrician she had seen privately when Gramps and Bonnie had thought she was on a shopping spree.

The waistband of the vivid scarlet needlecord jeans she had chosen soon wouldn't fasten round her middle. She laid a trembling hand over the small bulge, evidence of the precious new life that was growing inside her, and silently willed the unfounded dark pall of absolute terror to go away.

She had Aldo, had his love, and together they would see this through, Cat firmly reminded herself and felt immediately more secure and positive. She added a soft lambswool bright orange tunic top to give her back the courage she had momentarily lost, painted her lips a startling red and set off to find her hunky husband because being apart from him for ten minutes was proving to be ten minutes too long.

Her grandfather and Bonnie were taking their coats off in the hall as she walked down the stairs, their cheeks flushed with healthy colour from their walk in the fresh winter air.

Bonnie said, 'I'll go and make a start on lunch. Just a simple fish pie today.' She beamed cheerfully at Cat. 'Ask the *signor* if he'd like coffee. I'd ask him myself but he's just disappeared into the study with his mobile phone; I wouldn't want to disturb him.'

Another five minutes apart, Cat mourned, then sensibly decided she could just about manage that and said, 'I'm sure he'd like some. I'll help you, Bonnie.'

But Gramps said firmly, 'I want to talk to you in private, Caterina. I've been meaning to for some time now. The sitting room?'

Giving the housekeeper a wry, apologetic grin, Cat followed the remarkably spry figure of her grandfather into the sitting room, wondering what he needed to say that couldn't wait, and didn't find out because as soon as he'd settled himself in his favourite armchair at the side of the open fire Aldo walked into the cosy, chintzy room, his face lighting up with pleasure as his eyes homed in on her.

'I'll go and chase that coffee up,' the older man said tartly and unsettled himself again, stalking out of the room, and Aldo said, 'You are so bright and beautiful and I am so lucky.' And took her in his arms, wondering wryly, 'Was it something I did? Domenico is in a bad mood, yes?'

Nestling in the blissful comfort of his arms, Cat explained, 'It's nothing personal. He thinks you're Wonder Man with knobs on. He had something he wanted to say to me in private, but you walked in before he could come out with it.'

Unfazed, Aldo lifted her chin with a won't-take-no-for-an-answer forefinger and told her, 'If it's important we'll make sure he gets the privacy to get it off his chest before we have to leave,' and rained kisses on her eagerly responsive lips until she forgot all about it, and only when she remembered something else entirely did she pull away from him, look him straight in the eyes and tell him,

'Before we start on a new life together, I have a couple of conditions to make.'

'Conditions? You put conditions on the wonderful new life we are forging together?' His hands slid to her waist, pinioning her against him, his dark eyes gleaming with golden shafts of teasing light. 'I demand unconditional surrender!'

Gazing up into those laughter-filled eyes, the curving lines of his sensationally sexy mouth, Cat almost capitulated and vocalised the words of total surrender to his every whim that immediately sprang to mind.

Only when she had firmly reminded herself that now and then a woman—no matter how besotted she happened to be—had to show her man that she did have a mind of her own could she get out, 'I dress to please myself in future. I tried to look like a typically wealthy Italian's wife because I thought you'd expect it of me—tasteful designer gear in sophisticated, muted colours—and honestly it just wasn't me. I like bright things and—'

'You are the brightest thing in my life, *cara mia*,' he murmured softly. 'Whatever you wear you are beautiful. In fact,' still clasping her waist, he stepped back half a pace, his head tipped to one side as if in deep consideration, 'I definitely approve of those red trousers. Very sexy. And that orange top thing makes me very jealous.' His voice roughened hungrily. 'It touches your fabulous breasts. I want to change places with it.' His hands demonstrated his desire to do just that and Cat closed her hazy green eyes on a groan of uncontainable excitement, and when his mouth touched her parted lips she thought she might explode with the pleasure of what he could do to her.

Only reluctantly returning to reality when he stopped touching, stopped running tantalisingly soft kisses over her mouth and said wryly, 'Sadly, we must behave ourselves. You are tempting me to repeat our highly successful experiment of last night, *bella mia*! Think how we would embarrass your grandfather, and the estimable Bonnie would throw our coffee in the air and fall in a faint!'

He dropped one final kiss on the end of her nose and reminded her tenderly, 'Conditions, you said. Plural. So far you've only got around to talking about the way you intend to dress—which, by the way, I totally accede to.'

And whose fault was that? Taking a deep breath, Cat envied his control. She was still almost painfully aroused and she had to think really hard before she remembered what her other condition had been.

'You don't—' She stopped to clear the constriction in her throat then carried on a bit breathlessly. 'You don't leave me alone for weeks and weeks at a time. Oh, I do realise how hard you have to work,' she qualified rapidly, just in case he was thinking what a naggy, demanding wife she would turn out to be.

'And I appreciate that you made time to write funny postcards, and send gifts. But Aldo, I did miss you.'

She searched his gorgeous features for signs of male huffiness and found none, just frowning contrition.

He slapped a hand against the side of his head, and his voice was growly as he dragged her into his arms again, claiming rawly, 'I am an idiot! *Pazzo!* I had wanted to come to you and tell you I had put my working life in order, that I would be able to mostly conduct my business affairs by the touch of an electronic button from wherever we might happen to be. It was to be such a wonderful surprise!' he stated in a tone of sardonic self-deprecation.

He tilted her bright head back, his eyes dark and serious as they probed hers. 'You must have felt so neglected. I was too stupidly intent on what I was achieving to think of that! The way I saw it, I was working for a future that would allow us to spend all our time together, thinking you were getting all the pampering and luxury you needed after your miscarriage. Can you forgive me?' he pleaded. 'I had never been in love before. I was unused to conducting a love affair with my wife. I handled it very badly.'

He was asking her forgiveness!

Her mistakes had been far worse than his; he might have handled his 'surprise packet' badly but he'd had love in his heart, had been single-mindedly intent on achieving a closer future together for them both, while she had been crediting him with every sin she could think of!

Her eyes glistening with tears of contrition, Cat wound her arms around his neck and kissed him to stop him rubbing any more salt in the wound. And the kiss deepened to fiery passion and might have ended in goodness only knew what indiscretions had not Aldo ended it, alerted by her grandfather's un-subtle cough.

As always, Aldo kept his cool while Cat's head was still spinning wildly. At least Bonnie hadn't fainted! she thought, feeling her face go dark red as she hurriedly rearranged her clothing.

The coffee tray was safely deposited on a low table, and Aldo met the older man's twinkling eyes and said with smooth pride, 'You must excuse us. Cat has wonderful news. She is expecting our baby and we've never been happier!'

And wasn't that the truth! Cat thought mushily, her eyes fixed admiringly on his straight back and wide, rangy shoulders, on the arrogant way he held his perfectly shaped head, then felt herself drowning in the love that shone from his eyes as he turned back to her and took her hand.

And then they were both smothered in the warmest and sincerest congratulations, and champagne was produced to mark the occasion. Cat, contenting herself with a cup of weak coffee, wondered if there were any known cases of people actually exploding from sheer happiness.

It was all just a glorious blur until lunch was over and her grandfather said, just a little bit wistfully, 'Do you think you could both stay on until after Christmas? Bonnie and I would love to have you share it with us.'

'Cat?' Aldo turned to her, one dark brow slightly elevated.

He was leaving the decision down to her. But she knew what he wanted. And she knew Gramps would dearly love to have his family around him at this time of year and she would have loved to accommodate him—in spite of the way he'd disinherited her, whether she'd agreed to marry the man of his choice or not!

But, 'Sorry, Gramps. We need to get back to Florence. I need to arrange for regular check-ups, that sort of thing,' and was glad she'd made that decision when she saw the deep relief in Aldo's dark, dark eyes.

'Of course you must,' the old man agreed immediately. 'I was being selfish. Not thinking.' He reached over the table and patted her hand. 'Forget I mentioned it.'

'We want both you and Bonnie to be in Italy for the birth of our baby,' Aldo insisted. 'I'll make all the necessary travel arrangements—a car to collect you from here, the company's private jet. Early spring, if it suits you? Then you can enjoy the Italian

sun, get to really know your family again and wait
with us for the newest member to put in an appearance.'

They were due to return to Italy at the end of the
week. The days passed in a whirl of activity that Aldo
tried to calm down without a great deal of success.

There were gifts to be chosen and carefully
wrapped in shiny gold paper for Gramps, Bonnie and
Dan—not forgetting the cleaning lady, because Mrs
Peterson was proving herself to be a jewel beyond
price. And there was her packing to be done, the sale
of her equipment in the workshop to be arranged. The
Christmas tree to be ordered as usual, and collected
and set in the wide hallway. And decorated.

On the last afternoon Gramps was taking his usual
snooze in front of the sitting-room fire, Aldo was
helping Dan barrow the latest load of logs into the
woodshed and Cat was taking a rare break, sprawled
out on the chair on the other side of the hearth thinking cosy maternal thoughts, when her grandfather
snored and woke himself up.

'I'll make you a cup of tea, shall I?' Cat bounced
upright, knowing it was always the first thing he
wanted when he woke from his after-lunch nap.

But he waved her offer aside with, 'Mrs Peterson
always brings me a tray at four, just before she leaves,
as you very well know. And at least I've got you to
myself. There's something I want to say to you.'

He was beginning to look decidedly uncomfortable,
Cat thought, and she guessed that whatever he wanted

to say wouldn't be easy for him. She had never known her grandfather to be anything other than absolutely direct, never mincing his words if he thought that what he had to say was right.

Concerned, she padded over the hearth rug and sank down at his feet, laying her bright head against his knee. Just waiting.

'I don't want you to think badly of me, Caterina. What I did turned out for the best, didn't it? No, don't say anything,' he warned as she lifted her head, prepared to tell him she could never think badly of him. 'Just hear me out.'

He cleared his throat roughly then went quickly on, 'Ever since Aldo was a child my sister's letters were full of praise for his strong-minded character, his generosity and good humour. And the occasional photographs she let me have showed him to have the makings of a fine-looking man. I felt I knew him through and through.

'Then, after your dear grandmother died, I started thinking more and more often of my Italian family, to regret the irresponsible way I'd behaved as a young man. The ingratitude. The taking of handsome dividends I'd not lifted a finger to earn,' he sighed.

'I found myself with two definite aims. To make reparation and to hand your welfare and happiness over to the safekeeping of a man such as Aldo. I used blackmail. I'm not proud of it except in that it procured a happy result—I've never witnessed two peo-

ple more obviously in love with each other than you
and my great-nephew.

'What I do sincerely regret is having given you the
impression that I was completely cutting you off without the proverbial shilling. It wasn't so. I always intended those shares and whatever is left from the un-
earned dividends to return to the Patrucco family
business. But the rest—this house, your grandmother's jewellery—will be yours. Whatever had
happened—if you'd turned Aldo down flat, for in-
stance—I would never have left you with nothing. I
wanted you to know that. It's been bothering me, and
it's taken me too long to get round to it. But confessing my sins has never been my strong point!'

'Oh, Gramps!' Leaping to her feet, Cat leant over
his chair and gave him a huge hug. 'You and Gran
looked after me all my life. You were the only real
parents I had and you gave me a happy, secure childhood.' A fond kiss on each cheek. 'I would have still
loved you even if you'd thrown me out of the house
without a rag to my name—and don't you ever forget
it!' She grinned down at him. 'I might have been a
bit snippy when you told me you'd picked out a husband for me. But believe me, it couldn't have turned
out more beautifully!'

EPILOGUE

THE city of Florence sweltered beneath a sky so bright it hurt the eyes. The streets and squares were like ovens.

Fanning her face with a languid hand, Cat entered the nursery from the balcony, the full skirts of her pale cream-coloured fine-lawn dress whispering around her legs. A cluster of pale cream rosebuds nestled in her hair, just above one ear. She smiled widely. So many people today had told her she looked like a bride.

Her green eyes went dreamy as she checked the air-conditioning unit. The fact was, her gorgeous Aldo made her feel like a bride every day of her life!

And as for Gianluca Domenico Patrucco, well he was their precious bonus! Her lovely face wreathed in smiles, Cat quietly approached the carved-wood, lace-flounced crib which had been in the family for generations.

At just over two months old, her beautiful son bore a definite resemblance to his handsome father. All the doting attention he'd been receiving today had been lapped up with wide, gummy smiles and bubbly gur-gles, but as soon as he'd realised he was hungry the assembled guests had been treated to his world-beating lusty bellow.

Retreating to the nursery with her fist-flailing, scarlet-faced precious bundle of noise, Cat had removed the two-hundred-year-old christening gown, changed and fed him, and now he was sleeping like the darling little cherub that he was.

'All quiet.' Aldo had approached silently to join the fan club. 'Looks like an angel, doesn't he? It always surprises me how much noise can come from someone so small.'

One cream-coloured light-jacketed arm pulled her against the leanly elegant length of him and Cat looked up at him, her eyes adoring, her temperature sizzling as he traced a line of kisses from the point of her jawbone, all the way down her throat to the point of the V-neckline of her floaty dress.

'Have I ever told you how much I love you?'

His voice was low and luxuriously sexy and Cat answered breathlessly, 'A million times and still counting, but not to worry, I can never hear those words often enough.' She caught a wandering, tanned, long-fingered hand between her own and placed tender kisses on each of his knuckles and reminded him, 'Our guests.'

'Gone. Our son broke the party up pretty effectively!' He captured her hands and looped them around his neck, his dark eyes flirting with hers. 'I thanked them all for coming and made your excuses. I think some of the stuffier ones thought you should have handed our roaring offspring over to a hovering nanny! They were too polite to say so, of course, so I pointed out that we enjoy doing everything for him ourselves.'

So they did. Cat had been adamant that no hired nanny would take charge of her precious baby. And between them, she and Aldo had discovered that, despite the odd sleepless night, it was an adventure they wouldn't have missed for worlds.

Aware now that he was sneakily walking her towards their adjoining bedroom, Cat protested, definitely half-heartedly, 'Where are your parents?' She was very fond of them both, and it was mutual and she didn't want them to feel neglected on their final day here in Florence.

Aldo easily put her mind at rest. 'Out on the loggia, sitting in the shade with Domenico and Bonnie. My father's trying to persuade your grandfather to settle permanently near him in Amalfi. Bonnie, too. They are so used to each other. You know him better than anyone—do you think he's open to persuasion?'

'Maybe.' Cat couldn't think straight, not when her body was welded to the length of him. 'They've both been happy here in Italy, and I know Gramps feels as if he's come home at last. We'll have to wait and see.'

The bed was made of painted and gilded wood, with carvings of exotic birds and fruits. And whether the steamy heat was down to the ambient temperature or the sizzle of sexual excitement that arced between them, Cat couldn't say.

'Florence is too hot in August,' Aldo murmured as he gently turned her around and began sliding down the fine zip fastening at the back of her dress. Parting the fabric, he ran his fingers over her shoulder blades and down to her neat little waist. 'Tomorrow, after Bonnie and Domenico have been safely put aboard the jet for England and my parents have left for Amalfi, we will make plans to revisit Portofino.'

His hands retraced their path to her shoulders and the dress pooled to the floor. 'We will take Isabella and Louisa,' he named two of the permanent staff here in the Florence town house, 'to look after the villa and babysit on the evenings when I wine and dine my beautiful wife.'

He turned her round. She was wearing just a lacy bra and the tiniest of matching briefs. 'And you are so beautiful, *mi amore*. I am the luckiest man on the planet.'

And she was the luckiest woman in the universe, Cat thought as he shrugged out of his elegant jacket. She began a determined assault on the buttons of his shirt.

Eleven months later the two-hundred-year-old christening robe was in use again. Little Silvana Caterina behaved perfectly, following the proceedings with her mother's vivid green eyes, copper-coloured curls peeping out beneath her enchanting lace-trimmed bonnet while Gianluca was stomping around on his sturdy little legs, falling into the furniture because he hadn't got used to this walking business yet, his smart new sailor suit smeared with chocolate because he often missed where his mouth was.

Aldo had been over the moon at the arrival of the miniature of the woman he adored. 'But enough is enough,' he'd stated firmly. 'Two babies to keep us awake at nights, to have to watch like hawks. I am a greedy man. I want you to myself. The family christening robe gets locked away.'

'Just as you say, *caro mio*,' Cat had replied demurely as she lay with her newborn in her arms. 'We'll lock it away but we won't lose the key!'

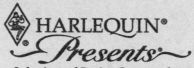

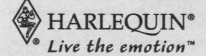

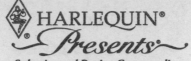

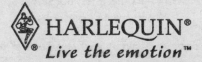